STAR TREK 49:
TRIANGLE

D1150280

STAR TREK NOVELS

1: CHAIN OF ATTACK
2: DEEP DOMAIN
3: DREAMS OF THE RAVEN
4: THE ROMULAN WAY
5: HOW MUCH FOR JUST THE PLANET?
6: BLOODTHIRST
7: THE I.D.I.C. EPIDEMIC
8: YESTERDAY'S SON
9: TIME FOR YESTERDAY
10: THE FINAL REFLECTION
11: TIMETRAP
12: THE VULCAN ACADEMY MURDERS
13: THE THREE-MINUTE UNIVERSE
14: *STAR TREK:* THE MOTION PICTURE
15: *STAR TREK:* THE WRATH OF KHAN
16: MEMORY PRIME
17: THE ENTROPY EFFECT
18: THE FINAL NEXUS
19: THE WOUNDED SKY
20: VULCAN'S GLORY
21: MY ENEMY, MY ALLY
22: DOUBLE, DOUBLE
23: THE COVENANT OF THE CROWN
24: CORONA
25: THE ABODE OF LIFE
26: ISHMAEL
27: WEB OF THE ROMULANS
28: THE CRY OF THE ONLIES
29: DREADNOUGHT
30: THE KOBAYASHI MARU
31: THE TRELLISANE CONFRONTATION
32: RULES OF ENGAGEMENT
33: THE KLINGON GAMBIT
34: THE PANDORA PRINCIPLE
35: THE PROMETHEUS DESIGN
36: DOCTOR'S ORDERS
37: BLACK FIRE
38: KILLING TIME
39: THE TEARS OF THE SINGERS
40: ENEMY UNSEEN
41: MINDSHADOW
42: HOME IS THE HUNTER
43: DEMONS
44: GHOST WALKER
45: MUTINY ON THE ENTERPRISE
46: A FLAG FULL OF STARS
47: CRISIS ON CENTAURUS
48: RENEGADE
49: TRIANGLE
Coming soon:
50: LEGACY

STAR TREK GIANT NOVELS

STRANGERS FROM THE SKY
FINAL FRONTIER
UHURA'S SONG
DWELLERS IN THE CRUCIBLE
SHADOW LORD
PAWNS AND SYMBOLS

A *STAR TREK*® NOVEL

TRIANGLE

SONDRA MARSHAK
AND
MYRNA CULBREATH

TITAN BOOKS
LONDON

STAR TREK 49: **TRIANGLE**
ISBN 1 85286 357 9

Published by
Titan Books Ltd
58 St Giles High St
London WC2H 8LH

First Titan Edition July 1991
10 9 8 7 6 5 4 3 2 1

British edition by arrangement with Pocket Books, a division of Simon
and Schuster, Inc., Under Exclusive Licence from Paramount Pictures
Corporation, The Trademark Owner.

Printed and bound in Great Britain by Cox and Wyman Ltd, Reading,
Berkshire.

TRIANGLE

Prologue

The Ambassador stood alone before the Federation Council. The Council knew, however, that the newly confirmed Ambassador to Zaran was never alone. He was One.

"I shall require the Enterprise to take my Oneness to Zaran," the Ambassador said.

"There is no route," the member from Andor said, "except through what the Humans call the Marie Celeste Sector—where every smaller ship has vanished."

"Yes. Therefore, I require the best starship."

A man rose in the chamber. He was the Chief of Staff of Starfleet. "It is your neck, Ambassador, but it is my starship."

The Ambassador nodded fractionally. "I would judge it is your neck, also. Your opposition to my mission to Zaran is known."

The Chief of Staff rose to his full height, which matched the Ambassador's. "That's right," he said. "I grant your right to the diversity of your Oneness, but I defend with my neck the right of every other diversity to exist. Zaran imposes Oneness by force. You have said nothing against that. I do not send the cub to guard the bear."

The Ambassador shrugged. "Do you send the amoeba to understand the man? Only a Oneness can hope to deal with a Oneness. But whether you or I like it or not, Oneness is coming to the galaxy. Whether by force or not, I do not know. The New Human movement now permeates your own planet. Collective consciousness is springing up everywhere. We are tomorrow."

"Or yesterday," the Chief of Staff said. "Perhaps a blind alley in evolution. There were many. No dinosaur ever knew that it was not a workable solution. You consider my people throwbacks, but it was those throwbacks who took us to the stars. And it is still old-fashioned love among solitary beings which keeps my ships going. I will give you the Enterprise, *where you may learn something extraordinary about that. Then tell me whether love, or Oneness, will keep us in the stars."*

The Ambassador smiled ironically. "Have you considered my servant Job?" he quoted.

There was a ripple of puzzlement in the chamber. "Translator context inadequate," the Andorian protested.

"It is not important," the Ambassador said. "Merely an ancient Human text said to report on a similar occasion. God's servant Job was the best; therefore, he was given to the Devil to test." He bowed to the Commander in Chief. "I accept, on the usual terms and conditions."

"What terms?" the Tellarite asked.

"That I may take his soul."

The Chief of Staff's eyes hardened. "Ambassador Gailbraith," he said, "I would give my right arm to command that ship myself. Failing that, there is one man I would trust to keep his soul from the Devil himself."

Gailbraith bowed fractionally. "Captain James T. Kirk. Unfortunately, the Devil will not be his adversary . . ."

Chapter 1

The solar system lay before them like a star traveler's dream: beautiful, untouched, a present from the universe, waiting to be unwrapped. Or a trap waiting to be sprung . . .

"The Cephalus system," First Officer Spock said from the *Enterprise* science station, "is the mathematical center of the Marie Celeste Sector. We must consider that it is a starship trap."

"Agreed, Mr. Spock," Kirk said. "Habitable planets?"

Captain James T. Kirk saw the Vulcan's dark head and pointed ears bend over the scanners, and he took advantage of Spock's concentration to move, too carefully, from near the turbolift doors to the command seat.

Not that there was much the Vulcan was going to miss about his Captain, or ever had, but the last thing Kirk wanted just now was for Spock to read whatever the hell was going on with his Captain. Fatigue, that was all. And a few half-healed injuries—ribs cracked and the like. He'd been banged up a little too much lately. And not getting much sleep, with those peculiar nightmares. Once, one of the nightmares had started to come by day . . . Suddenly, now, it came again . . .

> He was in some place where he was not alone, would never be alone again. Someone was with him who knew everything he was or wanted to be, and who was One with him, known to him, too—to the last secret. There was nothing more to be hidden or resisted. There were others, too, each one unique, but all now a part of him. And he knew now that they were a new life-form, struggling to be born. And, like any life-form, would have to grow, or die . . .

Kirk snapped himself out of it, realizing only then that he had slipped into that peculiar state again. It was a momentary feeling-state for which there were really no words. He was not certain why he felt such a depth of longing—so urgent, as if it had touched some inner, unknown core of loneliness. He was certain only that he had never felt anything like it, and never wanted to again.

And now he realized that he had had a moment's lapse on the Bridge.

That, he knew, could not properly be hidden from the Vulcan, who was his Second-in-Command.

Still he felt a curious reluctance to confess it.

Then Spock turned and Kirk saw that he had been read like Braille. The dark Vulcan eyes commented silently that the Human had unwrapped a few surprise packages too many lately, and sprung too many traps.

"The fourth planet," Spock said aloud, "is marginally Class-M, but extremely hazardous. There is a large satellite. And a very small one. Or a one-being ship in orbit."

"A one-man ship *here?*" Kirk said. *"That* would take more guts than brains."

"An excess which Humans have been known to demonstrate," Spock said pointedly.

"Whereas Vulcans, of course, only stick their stubborn necks out for perfectly logical reasons."

"Of course, Captain," Spock agreed blandly.

Kirk suppressed a grin and felt most of the fatigue drop away, which was doubtless what Spock had intended.

"Captain," Uhura said before Kirk could pursue a further Vulcan-routine, and Kirk heard a stress in her voice which made him turn to look at his Communications Officer. Her Bantu face was set in its usual beautiful discipline, but now with an anger which he could read.

"Ambassador Gailbraith is requesting a priority channel to the Federation Council to protest this delay and your behavior."

Kirk found himself trying to brace the cracked ribs, and stopped it. "Inform the Ambassador that he may have a channel to the Council when we are not under subspace silence. We are in the zone of ship disappearances which blocks travel to Zaran, as he knows."

"Yes, sir." Uhura started to turn back to her board. "Sir, may I make a personal observation?"

"Go ahead."

"Sir, the crew doesn't understand Ambassador Gailbraith and his party. Some of them have been pressuring our people to join their 'Oneness'—they don't seem to take 'no' for an answer. The crew's starting to say: 'Are *these* the New Humans? Are *they* what we're supposed to be out here for—or what we are supposed to *become?*'"

Kirk smiled ruefully. "I don't 'reach' the Ambassador and company too well myself. I'm not sure whether his party would call themselves New Humans. But they do seem to be part of a growing trend toward submerging the individual in a larger consciousness. If they're the future, I suppose we are the past. But I wouldn't bet that it isn't the other way around."

"But they're going to *Zaran,* sir—and they act as if they are going *home.*"

KIrk did not smile now. He had made some efforts to consider the point of view by which he and his kind—Spock, McCoy, Uhura, the *Enterprise* crew and all of Starfleet—were more or less prehistoric throwbacks to an outdated age of individualism. But he did not, finally, believe it.

And that New Human view had nearly cost him the stars. The New Humans had little real use for Starfleet, and to overcome their growing influence, Commanding Admiral

Heihachiro Nogura had wanted to keep Kirk on Earth as a live hero and a living argument for Starfleet. He had caught Kirk at a vulnerable moment at the end of the first five-year mission, and the result was the three years Kirk had spent at the Admiralty—learning that he could not live there.

If he had not seized on the Vejur crisis as an opportunity to regain command of the *Enterprise,* he would have been there still—or at least until Earth was destroyed by Vejur. Spock, theoretically, would have embraced the total non-emotion of Kolinahr in the mountains of Gol.

Somehow Kirk had never expected the philosophy of One to follow him into the spaces between the stars, at least not in this form.

The Ambassador and his party looked like normal Humans with a sprinkling of other species, but shared some form of Oneness he did not understand. He had learned to live with and appreciate many diversities. This one made him acutely uncomfortable, and he was realizing now that perhaps that discomfort was part of his own curious fatigue. He snapped himself back to the immediate problem.

"The Ambassador's philosophy is not our concern," he said. "We are merely ordered to get him to Zaran."

"Eventually," Uhura said under her breath, and Kirk saw Weapons Officer Pavel Chekov give her a long look.

"Uhura," Kirk said, "we have received no political orders."

"No, sir," Uhura said stoutly. "Of course not." She did not add that they had been ordered to investigate two unknown solar systems and a years-old unsolved mystery of disappearing ships *en route.* There was a policy there somewhere.

"You will relay my message to the Ambassador," Kirk said. "I will see him when convenient."

"Yes, sir."

Kirk turned back to Spock.

"The scoutship," Spock said, "is in landing approach to the fourth planet."

"Uhura," Kirk said, "raise that scout. Warn it of extremely hazardous planet conditions. What's it like down there, Mr. Spock?"

"Think of it as an Earth of a million years ago. There are wild extremes—heat, cold, rain, drought, jungle, volcanoes, predators. And it is in a stage of gigantism such as Earth had.

The life-form readings are much larger than one would expect."

"How much larger?" Kirk asked, suspecting that he did not want to know.

Spock shrugged. "Remember the Oiduvai Gorge findings? Africa, mid-twentieth century. A Dr. Leaky found bones of *sheep* which stood twelve feet high at the shoulder—with six-foot spans of horses. There were predators to match. Also one primitive humanoid, about our size—who died at an early age."

Kirk grinned, finding that kind of problem really much more to his taste. "Mr. Spock, you are a tower of strength and encouragement."

"Captain," Uhura said, "I can't raise the scout, but it sent off a micro-burst of high-speed code as it went down. We can't read it, but I recognize the type. It's an idiosyncratic memory code of the kind used only by a Free Agent of the Federation."

"A Free Agent!" Kirk found himself on his feet, the fatigue falling away at the prospect of action. "Plot the landing trajectory, Mr. Sulu, and relay the landing coordinates to the Transporter Room. Mr. Spock, come with me."

Spock followed him into the turbolift.

"VIP Guest Quarters," Kirk said to the voice control.

"I will call a transporter party," Spock began.

"We are the party, Mr. Spock—as soon as I have a word with Ambassador Gailbraith."

"Doctor McCoy specified light duty after your last injuries."

Kirk shrugged. "A stroll on the planet, Mr. Spock. The air will do me good." Spock started to protest, but he cut it off. "That's a Free Agent down there, Spock, and that signal was almost certainly some call for help. A Free Agent doesn't break idiosyncratic code silence for much less than a world coming to an end."

Spock nodded. "The call, however, was not to us."

"Nevertheless, we're going in. We would offer assistance to any lone traveler on a world like that—and check out any lone figure in a suspicious sector. If we did less, it would only be because we know it is a Free Agent. If anybody is watching . . ."

He stopped as the turbolift deposited them near the VIP

Guest Wing. "A Free Agent. You know, Spock, if I have any heroes . . ."

There had been only a handful of full-fledged Free Agents in Starfleet history. They answered to no one except the Old Man himself—not even to Commanding Admiral Nogura, but to the Chief of Staff of Starfleet. They could and did hold the power of peace and war, reform and revolution. Not one man in a billion had that kind of mind and nerve and terrible independence. And most who had ever held that rank had died in it. Young.

"Starship captains," Spock said, "seldom survive a five-year mission."

Kirk looked at him, startled, as if the Vulcan had read his thought. "That's different," he said.

Spock nodded dispassionately. "Yes. It is harder."

Kirk found himself unreasonably touched. But he was in no condition to pursue it. He set himself and went through the double doors into the VIP Lounge.

Chapter 2

The gray weight of fatigue settled on Kirk again. He saw the Ambassador and his party, perhaps thirty of them, standing in a circle, each with a hand touching the back of the neck or base of the skull of the next one. They wore short white-belted robes, some over dark tights. They were men and women—predominantly young, but centered around a powerful figure of authority: Gailbraith. Their eyes were closed and the aura of some contact between them was almost palpable, even to Kirk. He could have held that sense of contact in his hands. Or perhaps it could have held *him* . . .

He saw his First Officer react to it with the sensitivity of Vulcan attunement to telepathy, and Spock's reaction was to step in front of Kirk with something blazing from his dark eyes which Kirk had not seen before.

The Ambassador's eyes opened and locked with Spock's, and now Kirk could sense the unified power of the Oneness directed toward himself. Then he could sense the Vulcan's mental fight against it.

Kirk felt shockingly drained, and suddenly he wondered if this could be having some effect on him beyond his own fatigue and half-healed injuries. But if it affected *him*—what would it do to a born telepath?

Kirk stepped forward himself and stepped in between the Ambassador and Spock. The circle parted and Kirk crossed to confront Gailbraith. Eyes popped open around the group, and some carrier-wave was broken. Some of the group remained to watch their meeting, and some drifted off.

"Ambassador," Kirk said, "you are, of course, welcome to practice your customary mental disciplines on this ship, so long as you respect the rights of other beings. However, we have a number of species aboard who are sensitive in some way to mental emanations. I do not expect you to use your Oneness to broadcast hostility, ill will, or attempts to prose-lytize."

The Ambassador shrugged. He was tall, broad-shouldered, of an aristocratic bearing, gray-eyed, his face carved out of some crag. He was perhaps the last man anyone would have suspected as a candidate for Oneness. If an artist had looked for a model of rugged individualism, he would have picked that face.

"Oneness is our life," Gailbraith said. "We-the-One in-clude both love and anger. We cannot be ordered not to be One for all our purposes."

"On my ship," Kirk said, "you will confine yourself to purposes compatible with your Ambassadorial mission, with the mission of this ship—and with the well-being of its crew."

"On this Federation ship," the Ambassador said, "you will not delay an Ambassador of the Federation in the assumption of his rightful duties. Whether you are acting on orders in these delays or on your own initiative and prejudice, I will carry the matter all the way to the Federation Council. You—and the source of your orders, however high—will answer to a board of inquiry, together with anyone who abets you . . ." He looked at Spock.

"Then I will answer to a board of inquiry," Kirk said, "but you will not disrupt my ship."

"Captain," the Ambassador said, "you are a dinosaur. Obsolete. A dying species. You have had your day, and now the day is ours. You can be replaced. And you will be."

"Can I?" Kirk said. "Do you really believe that a collective could run this ship—or build her? The *Enterprise* flies on single thoughts from single minds, from the first man who tamed fire to the last one who tamed the fire of a starship."

The Ambassador smiled fractionally. "Are you certain, Captain? What if that individual creativity springs from a collective unconscious? What if your own strength as a commander comes from a unique unity? Your command crew is celebrated as having a rapport unmatched in Starfleet. What, Captain, if *you* are *us?*"

Kirk shook his head. "I'm not. We are not. Our kind of rapport is based on nothing more than an old four-letter word. Obsolete—but not extinct."

"Love, Captain? It is a fable—unless it is the love of Oneness, of the other as self. And if it *is*, then you *are* us." He looked at Spock. "Or do you claim that your ship has taught even a Vulcan to love?"

"Mr. Spock is what he is," Kirk said. "He is not a subject for discussion. I merely came to inform you that we will be detained, briefly, I trust, while I investigate the center of the starship disappearances. We will maintain subspace silence until we are through the dangerous sector. Until then you will confine your objections to my actions to direct statements to me, and keep your hostility and your zeal to your individual selves."

The Ambassador shook his head. "Captain Kirk, you are in many ways an admirable specimen of a limited species. But you must accept your own limitations. Could an amoeba understand the simplest multicelled animal? Would it ask that animal to disassemble itself periodically into its individual cells? Would it know that that would be death?"

For a moment Kirk looked at him, wondering. The Ambassador and his party still *looked* like individual beings. The temptation was to assume that they *were* merely that—perhaps with some modest mental link. But what if they really were a living thing, a new thing under the sun . . . ? What if he *was* the amoeba?

"Ambassador," Kirk said, "I am prepared to consider the possibility that you have something. What I am not prepared to do is to see it imposed by force, physical or mental. Not on Zaran. And not here."

Gailbraith looked at him with steel-gray appraising eyes. "Captain, the first multicelled animals must have absorbed a great many amoeba—curtailed their freedom, violated their individual amoeba rights. Doubtless the amoeba protested. But butterflies were born, and tigers, and men."

Kirk shook his head. "A man is not an amoeba. The argument of the good of the many or the good of the superior being has been made before—by every dictatorship."

"A dictatorship is not a Oneness. You would not know, Captain, until you have been a Part-Whole." He bowed fractionally. "I will show you."

He put his hand up toward Kirk. The forefinger parted from the other three in a *V*—not the Vulcan sign of paired fingers, but the hand sign of One, set apart from the Unity. Kirk knew it was an invitation to match it, palm to palm, and to share—thought? Feeling? Oneness?

There had been many times when he had not backed away from some form of mental contact—the Vulcan mind-meld, occasionally some other sharing. He was not set against the new, or he would not have been out here. But his deepest instinct rebelled against this—and he saw Spock's face set against it, almost as if he would move to intervene. Then the Vulcan did speak.

"Captain," Spock said, "I must point out that your exposure to an unknown, powerful group mental effect could require me to assume command."

Kirk measured the depth of the Vulcan's resistance by his willingness to say that in front of the Ambassador. "Mr. Spock is quite correct, Ambassador," Kirk said immediately. "No. Thank you. If I were not in command, possibly. I could afford the luxury."

Gailbraith smiled. "No, Captain, you could not."

Kirk looked at him and revised an estimate. There was something dangerous about the man, and something which could not be dismissed.

"Be that as it may, Ambassador, you and your people will refrain from drawing any member of my crew into a Part-Whole demonstration of any kind. Good day, Ambassador."

Kirk turned to leave. From around the corner of an alcove where some of Gailbraith's party had wandered off Kirk heard a peculiar strangled sound—not quite a scream. A man's scream.

He and Spock moved as one, charged through the alcove doors—

And saw Mr. Dobius, the seven-foot Tanian with bifurcated head—who could give Spock's Vulcan strength a workout —held by a slender girl.

It was a moment before they saw that the white-robed girl matched Mr. Dobius' big hand in the One-apart gesture the Ambassador had offered Kirk. Her other hand reached up to the back of Dobius' neck, and it was as if a current flowed which Dobius could not break. She was moving their separated forefingers toward a joining with the Unity of the other fingers.

"She must not complete the joining!" Spock snapped.

Kirk was a fraction ahead and couldn't have agreed more. He reached to pull the girl's hand away from Dobius.

He might as well have locked onto durasteel. Suddenly he sensed the power flowing through her—not her own but the power of a Oneness. Even as he had spoken to the Ambassador, the multiheaded Oneness had also been doing its work here.

Spock did not try to move the woman, even with his Vulcan strength. But he lifted Dobius bodily and flung him clear. The Tanian crumpled against a bulkhead.

And the girl turned on Kirk. For a moment he tried to ward her off gently. Then her hands closed on his temples and he could feel the flow of a current which somehow included the Ambassador and a lurching Copernican Revolution in the way Kirk saw things, as if indeed the amoeba saw that the Oneness was always at the center of things . . .

Kirk tried to hurl himself back, then felt chivalry go and tried simply to break her hold. But his arms were lead, his legs were melting . . .

Spock's hands closed on him and also lifted Kirk bodily away and around behind him as Spock turned to face the girl—and the Ambassador and his party who had come in behind her.

"That will do, Viana," the Ambassador said quietly. "The Vulcan has his own disciplines."

The green-eyed girl appraised Spock momentarily and bowed her head slightly. "A pity," she said.

Behind Spock Kirk felt in astonishment that his legs were failing him. He was crumpling to the deck. Suddenly it was not Spock but Gailbraith who moved—past Spock and locking on to Kirk's arm with one hand. It was not a way in which a man could stop another man from falling—even the Vulcan would not have tried it. And yet Kirk felt himself held up, lifted, supported as if by a living power which flowed into him through the touch. Then Spock turned and from somewhere Kirk managed to lock his legs into position and straighten away from Gailbraith's hold. It was like disconnecting a life-support system. For a moment Kirk crumpled against the wall. Spock moved in, but Kirk waved him off and reached for the intercom.

"Effective immediately," he said, "the Ambassador and his party will confine themselves to the VIP Guest Areas. There will be no fraternization with the *Enterprise* crew. Kirk out."

"You would deny a Federation Ambassador the freedom of a Federation starship?" Gailbraith said.

Kirk drew himself up. "I have known Federation Ambassadors of the stature of Sarek of Vulcan," he said. "Never have I known one who would order or condone the imposition of unwanted mental contact on an unwilling being. I intend to take *that* to the Federation Council."

Mr. Dobius came up to stand before Kirk. A Tanian, Kirk decided, should not attempt to look sheepish.

"Sir," Dobius said, "I have to report—I wasn't entirely unwilling. I just—I believe your expression would be—'got in over my head.' Sir."

Kirk looked up at him. "Mr. Dobius, you got in over both our heads—which in your case should have been rather more difficult. Report to Doctor McCoy."

"I'm all right, sir."

"You have been in mental contact with an alien life-form, Mr. Dobius. Report."

"Yes, sir."

Kirk turned back to Gailbraith. "My order stands. There is no being on this ship, with the possible exception of Mr. Spock, who could be certain of standing against your Oneness. But I will see that no one is obliged to try." He nodded to Spock. "See that the doors close, Mr. Spock."

He saw the Vulcan advance on the Ambassador's party as

if the peaceable Vulcan only wished the Ambassador would not step back. But the Ambassador's party saw something in Spock's eyes which must have made them decide against pushing their luck.

They stepped back and the doors closed in front of them. Spock pushed a lock signal.

He turned in time to catch Kirk's shoulders as he sagged.

But after an instant Kirk straightened against the wall and waved Spock off. "Don't fuss over me, Mr. Spock. I'm not quite a lost cause yet."

Spock's look did not soften. "Captain, I recommend you give me the con and report to Doctor McCoy."

Kirk pried himself off the wall. "In that case *you* would have to face Gailbraith's board of inquiry."

Spock shrugged.

Kirk grinned. "And you would do me out of a perfectly good outing to meet a Free Agent." He was able to walk more steadily now. "Transporter Room, ten minutes."

"Captain," Spock said, "you have been in mental contact with an alien being."

Kirk stopped. "Yes, Mr. Spock. I have." He looked at Spock. "Not for the first time, Spock." He turned away abruptly. "Ten minutes."

He could feel the Vulcan's eyes boring into his back.

Chapter 3

Dr. McCoy looked up to see Spock entering Sickbay wearing a look McCoy read as trouble, big trouble.

McCoy left Dobius on the diagnostic table with Chapel and gestured Spock into his private office.

"No physiological damage to Dobius that we can pinpoint," McCoy said.

"And mental damage?" Spock asked.

McCoy shrugged. "I doubt we'll detect any, but then—how would we know what to look for? There's not a lot of research on the new collective-consciousness entities. They themselves are not much interested. Or maybe they know in their own way without research. And we 'singletons' don't know where to begin."

"Doctor," Spock said, "you had better find out. The

Captain has just had mental contact with such a collective-consciousness or multiple-life-form. I suspect now that he may have been under some mental pressure from it even before."

"*What?*" McCoy said.

"Doctor, it is pointless to try to keep the Captain's medical condition from me. He just collapsed in front of me."

McCoy reached for his med-kit. "In front of *you?* Then it's worse than I thought."

Spock stopped him. "Not yet. What is it?"

McCoy faced him squarely now. "Spock, I don't know. Stress, of course. You can kill anything by making it get ready to fight or run too often. Even a Starship Captain. But that doesn't seem to account for it fully. Sure, he was banged up lately on a few missions. God knows he's taken a terrible beating for years. But he's always bounced back. Now—" He shook his head.

Spock straightened. "Doctor, you and I have seen him hurt worse and under more stress. We have never seen him stopped. I suggest you consider what I suggested. An alien effect."

"But damn it, Spock," McCoy exploded, "to what purpose? And if it *were* from Gailbraith's party—what would we do about it?"

"Doctor," Spock said, "there is no public figure in the galaxy more resistant to the New Humans and other collectives' philosophies and life-styles than a Starship Captain—especially *this* Starship Captain, who is now known to the immediate galaxy. What would happen if Captain James T. Kirk became a New Human?"

McCoy looked at him incredulously. "Never happen, Spock. Not *him.*"

"Leonard," Spock said gravely, "his own natural mental shielding has been eroded by necessary mental contact with aliens over the years, including me. Once or twice he has reached me spontaneously. Recently something has lowered his shields further. Possibly it is a cumulative effect. And possibly now it is a mental assault from Gailbraith's party. Unless I shield, I can feel the Captain's pain now. An immense weariness . . . a resistance to some pressure he cannot name . . . a wish for something he cannot have . . ."

Spock turned away. For a moment he stood with hands

locked behind his back. Then he turned back to McCoy. "You cannot know the hunger for unity which can exist in one whose island self has begun to taste it, only to be cut off again."

McCoy stared at him, but Spock was moving toward the door. "I suggest that you perpetrate one of your famous deceptions, Doctor. 'Wangle' yourself an invitation to this landing party."

McCoy grabbed the med-kit and bolted after Spock. He tried to match the Vulcan's stride in the hall. "God damn it, Spock. You can't leave me hanging with that. Are you saying that your contacts with Jim, among other things, may have left him vulnerable to being absorbed by a collective?"

"I believe that is what I *said*."

"I don't buy it, Spock. He's the last man in the galaxy—"

"Doctor, he is the first. He always has been. If he has not so much explored inner space, it is because stars were at his feet. Now he has seen the strange new worlds. He has lost more than most men ever attempt—lost loves, lost friends, lost enemies. He has tasted forbidden fruit. And he has walked out on Eden, more than once. What if, once, he did not?"

Spock turned then, without a further word, into the Transporter Room.

Chapter 4

Kirk started to head for his cabin, then changed his mind. It was the first place Spock—or McCoy—would look, and his need now was to be alone.

Also, if he ever stopped—sat down, lay down—he was not sure how he would get moving again. He had perhaps ten minutes before the scout would be down and the coordinates available.

"Pool One," he said to the turbolift in abrupt decision. Moments later the turbolift decanted him in the small Pool/Gym One—by common consent, though not by rule, normally used only by the command crew, occasionally by VIP guests. But it would be locked off from Gailbraith's contingent now by the isolation-lock Spock had thrown. The lock was used occasionally to isolate the VIP Quarters as a quarantine ward or isolation quarters for an inimical alien life-form.

That, Kirk thought, was quite possibly what they had aboard . . .

The Pool area was empty.

He stepped into a sonic shower and let its transporter dissolve his clothes away and do its revival program, which was virtually guaranteed to raise the dead. It played him an Alpha-Hypno tape as it did it, which assured him vocally and subliminally that he was feeling fine, better than before, better and better.

It lied.

He programmed for swimming and the transporter device obligingly draped him in net briefs and a towel. He went out and gave himself to the water. He did a lazy backstroke, little more than floating, but it would take some of the knots out of him. God knew how he could have been so deeply affected by that momentary touch of Oneness, but even now he felt empty, ravaged, and indelibly *alone* . . .

Suddenly his body convulsed around a cramp so massive that he could neither breathe nor move. It doubled him into a ball and his face was under water. His arms and legs went into spasm. He held his breath and made desperate efforts to pull toward the surface, the side of the pool. But he knew he wasn't making it.

What was it they said about never swimming alone? Damn fool. "Starship Captain Drowns in Bathtub . . ."

Part of a Oneness would not die that way—

Maybe he sent a kind of call. He was never certain . . .

He had held breath to the point beyond unconsciousness.

From some deep point of awareness he felt a massive strength reach him and lift him to the surface, move him with long strokes to the side of the pool and lift him with one arm up onto the side.

He began to relax then. There was only one strength of that kind on the *Enterprise,* and he was safe in its hands.

He felt breath pumped into his lungs and strong hands began to unknot the cramp. Then his lungs fought for breath and found their own rhythm, and the hands merely focused on making the spasmed muscles relax all over his body.

Oddly, he felt a curious kind of warmth flowing from the

hands, as if an overabundance of vitality were channeled directly into him. His knotted muscles eased, and some deeper level of pain seemed to ease, too.

Spock was always coming up with some new rabbit out of his Vulcan hat . . .

The warmth moved up Kirk's body to his face, his temples, and he felt a soothing, lulling flow of energy, an invitation, a welcome, an end to aloneness, a limitless vista, as if he looked through some great compound-eye, onto uncounted separate views of stars and faces, landscapes, and distant places . . . And within it all somewhere, one mind, shockingly powerful, with a plan for the galaxy.

He could not see the plan, but it was complex and subtle, based on observations made, inferences drawn, brilliant leaps of speculative logic and prediction. Somehow he saw a visual of the pattern of it, a great three-cornered battle, in which he and his were at one point, and two other great opposing forces were at the other two. Each of the opposing forces was a Oneness, the first controlled by one planner he knew, and the other by some force yet unknown. He did not find that strange. He saw a brilliant plan which overreached him. And somehow he had expected it.

What he had not expected was the seductive appeal of this merging. It would be so easy just to let go, accept, become a mind with a thousand eyes. Yes, and a thousand bodies, tuned to each other, sharing sensation and sensuality, forfeiting nothing—except perhaps some amoeba singularity.

For a long moment it seemed simple, natural, a direction of growth, and he moved easily to look out through one set of eyes, one facet of the great compound-eye of a new creature.

He looked down into his own face.

His face was pale and drawn. Long-fingered hands held it and gave it some urgent flow of life-force. For a moment he could look out also through the mind behind those eyes, appraising the contours of his face, the state of his being, the stubbornness of his resistance, the vulnerability of his solitude . . .

Kirk wrenched himself back then and fought fiercely to recapture his own single consciousness, fought his way up through levels and layers, and finally opened his own eyes.

It was Gailbraith who knelt over him.

The Ambassador had, clearly, refused to stay behind

locked doors. And he had thrown off his white robe and Ambassadorial dignity to save his adversary's life.

The gray eyes looked down at Kirk with absorbed interest, as if studying the lines of his face. The hands continued to massage the muscles of his arms, sending the flow of warmth through them.

From somewhere, as though it were a carrier-wave, Kirk could sense the flow of a vast pool of life-energy which the tall man could tap at will.

"Thank you," Kirk said when he could speak. "That will be enough."

One hand moved deftly to release a knot in his neck, then stopped. "You *are* welcome," Gailbraith said.

"A little too welcome, possibly." He understood only too well that if the man wanted to claim his reward now and press his advantage, there was probably no strength by which Kirk could resist. And there was some enemy within which possibly even wanted it. Was this the way in which he was going to be initiated into Oneness?

"Ambassador," Kirk said quietly, "I thank you for my life. I am inclined to pay my debts. But the payment which I assume you want—is not mine to give."

"Whose is it?"

Kirk merely shook his head. "Call it—a prior obigation—to my ship, my crew, my friends."

"Your Vulcan friend?"

"I owe him, alone, my life, dozens of times over. If there were nothing else, I could not do it for that."

Gailbraith nodded fractionally. "And yet you must always be locked in separate cages. Or so you believe. Except in those moments when the call of duty has required you to share minds. Captain, you regard my Oneness with distrust, distaste. Did you find those moments of Oneness—distasteful?"

"No."

"Or the moment you just shared?"

For a moment Kirk was silent. "No," he said. "But I did not choose it, and I do not choose it."

"You will."

"Ambassador, I do not take easily to being taken over or forced. Conceivably you could take me into your Oneness without my consent, if I were weakened enough. I do not advise it. I would destroy you."

Gailbraith smiled. "The thought has occurred."

"I sensed—a plan. A galaxy-spanning plan. Yours?"

"Captain," Gailbraith said, "this is the age of the mutation of Oneness. I-the-Many am not the only One. I have my plan. I know of at least one other Oneness, which plans, ultimately, on a galactic scale."

"Who?" Kirk asked. "Or—*what?*"

"Did you suppose that the Human conquerors of Zaran brought with them only the physical technology of the old totalitarian empires of Earth? No. They brought also the psychic technology which was researched first there. And with both they conquered an ancient species of great power which had never been defeated. The native Zarans had a power of Oneness, rare but very strong. Now it is being used by the ruthless. The time may come, Captain Kirk—and before long—when you will have to choose my Oneness, or theirs."

Kirk struggled to sit up, and Gailbraith lifted him with one steely hand. "Ambassador," Kirk said, "I have found that when I am offered a choice of the lesser evil, it is still evil."

He made it to his feet on his own and stood there swaying. "My life is here."

Gailbraith smiled. "I have made something of a study of what you require for your life, Captain. Rather more than you have made yourself. It is quite possible that you will find what you have not known you needed on this trip—perhaps even on the planet below, where you hope that I do not know whom you will meet. I know. And I know what that one needs, also. For that reason you will play out the script I have written for you. There is no escape. But I shall enjoy the process of seeing you try."

"Why me?" Kirk said.

The gray eyes seemed to inspect them to his soul. "There are many obvious reasons, Captain. You are the epitome of your kind, the best of your breed, the hope of singletons everywhere. You are the prime target of the other side." He smiled rather oddly. "None of that is my primary reason."

"What is?"

The gray eyes looked through him. "Perhaps you remind

me of someone. Did you suppose that I became a Oneness without fighting it virtually to the death?"

Kirk looked at him intently. "I hadn't considered it. You still don't say that that *is* your reason."

"You notice that?"

"Ambassador, you will excuse me. I am expected."

"Yes," Gailbraith said, and for the first time the gray eyes seemed to laugh. "You *are.*"

Kirk turned away, but his legs failed him. He found Gailbraith supporting him by a hand. Then the man's other hand touched his temple.

Presently he felt much better. He walked away, not looking back, stopped at the sonic shower to program clothes, and went to keep his appointment with Spock. It seemed to him that there was something important which he should remember. He could not, at the moment, think *what* . . .

Chapter 5

McCoy saw Spock give up a fruitless search for Kirk. Abruptly he became aware that he had never—well, not for years—seen Spock search fruitlessly for Kirk. Unless some alien interference had cut off the "carrier wave" of some kind of empathy which they seemed to have between them. . . .

Abruptly he became aware that he was missing something from Spock himself. McCoy had always contended that he had about as much psionic sensitivity as a potato. That was a pretty good cover. And it might even be true, given that plants shriveled when you directed hostile thoughts at them, and vice versa. But he had been aware for years that he tended to bask in the Vulcan's presence. Whereupon, of course, he made it a point to bristle. Now whatever it was that he basked in was shut down.

"Spock," he said, "you're not *there*. And you can't find him. Have you—closed up shop—to keep him from feeling something?"

Spock turned to him and his look was suddenly savage. "You will cease to pry into my personal affairs, Doctor!"

He turned and strode toward the Transporter Room, leaving McCoy to follow in his wake with alarm bells going off.

They met Kirk at the door and went through it without even comment, although McCoy saw Kirk flash Spock a "later for you" look for bringing McCoy. The Vulcan seemed oblivious. But he inspected Kirk closely, and evidently did not like what he saw. Personally McCoy thought Kirk looked better than they had any right to expect. He must have gone through some mental discipline of his own and banished most of the weakness and fatigue. You didn't survive as a Starship Captain without having a pretty fair selection of mind-body techniques and Alpha-hypno routines. But McCoy knew this man's mind and body better than he knew his own—and paid far more attention to them. He saw the underlying stress, perhaps worse than he had ever seen it.

And there was some new abstracted look which he didn't like at all.

He pulled out his spray hypo.

"Not now, Bones." Kirk waved him off.

"Who's the doctor around here?" McCoy grumbled and continued to set the hypo.

"Who's the Captain?" Kirk shot back. "Mr. Spock, is it possible you are bucking for *both* jobs?"

"Neither," Spock said stiffly. Then he seemed to make a massive effort to rise to the occasion. "However, I believe Doctor McCoy has complimented me on my bedside manner."

"Doubtless," Kirk said. "The two of you make a pair."

McCoy attached himself to an arm and shot the spray hypo home. Mega-vitamins and mild stimulants, and mild neurotransmitter normalizers. He didn't dare try more. If Spock was right, more stress could just push Kirk over the edge. And he wished he had a normalizer for Spock. He saw Kirk look at the Vulcan and not much like how he looked. But he was still irritated that Spock had dragged McCoy into it.

"I don't recall inviting *you*, Bones," Kirk complained.

"Scuttlebutt," McCoy said, "has it that you're going down there after a Free Agent. I've never met one. Mind if I tag along?"

Kirk sighed with his look of missing nothing. "Maybe I *need* a nursemaid." He gestured McCoy toward the transporter.

But the outer doors opened and a Communications Yeoman came in. "An 'eyes only' command-code transmission, Captain."

"Thank you, Yeoman. Dismissed." The Yeoman turned on his heel and left. Kirk snapped the seal, read the brief message. McCoy saw surprise register in his face, then a kind of shock.

He looked up at Spock and McCoy. "You might as well hear this. 'Effective immediately *Enterprise* is placed at disposal of Free Agent 7-10.' It's signed by the Chief of Staff."

"But that would be giving the Free Agent the ultimate authority over the ship," McCoy said.

Kirk's jaw was set. "Exactly, Bones."

"Must be hell's own crisis," McCoy said. "Or the Old Man wouldn't put you in that position."

"We've had some tough ones lately. What if somebody is beginning to figure I've had it?"

"Nuts, Jim. They know you."

"*Spock* knows me—and he headed straight off to bring the doctor along."

"Captain—" Spock began.

"Never mind, Mr. Spock. You've made your point. Probably correctly. For your information, gentlemen, I have had waking nightmares lately in which I—or someone who might have been me—was drawn to Oneness. Let's go."

A security man entered with equipment Kirk must have ordered earlier. Bio-belts with heavy hand phasers. And McCoy noted that there were already three of them. Maybe he had been invited, after all. Kirk knew damn well he needed McCoy now if that was happening to him—and not only as doctor.

Kirk flashed him an expression which had a trace of the old mischief in it, and McCoy felt unaccountably better. Whatever the stresses and strains, this still wasn't a man who came apart.

"Set phasers on heaviest stun and bio-belts on three," Kirk said.

McCoy raised an eyebrow. "That would ignore everything but some pretty large animals, wouldn't it? *What* is down there?"

"We're about to find out. Energize."

Chapter 6

The bio-belts were supposed to give you eyes in the back of your head—also neck and other anatomy. Directional sensors projected their biological readings directly on the nerves of the skin.

The party beamed down into a jungle clearing where biological warning systems were obviously the first need of survival. But the bio-belts immediately set up such a clamor that they had eyes in every inch of skin. The neuro-dermal circuits which made the skin crawl in the direction of an approaching animal went crazy.

The planet's surface was a biological soup—thick with life, boiling with activity, and smelling of danger.

McCoy saw an animal scurry through the tall grass with the

tiny timorousness of a mouse. It sat up and twitched its nose at him. It was the size of a medium dog.

"If those are the *mice*—we won't have to worry about the tigers and the *snarths*," McCoy groused. "The pussycats can carry us off."

As if in answer, there was a low roar which sounded like a saber-toothed tiger made out in triplicate.

"In this form of gigantism," Spock said dispassionately, "the predators may not be quite as oversized as the plant-eaters."

"Well, *that's* a comfort," McCoy grumbled.

Enormous shadows and mysterious rumblings moved just outside the dense edge of the clearing. McCoy caught a flash of green-yellow horizontal cat-eyes. Very large. Some of the trees appeared to be interconnected, with multiple trunks and interlaced branches.

"Reduce bio-belt setting to six," Kirk ordered.

They turned to inspect the battered interstellar scoutship which had come down in the clearing. It had seen better days, and somebody had recently shot it up. But what looked like repairs jury-rigged in space had held it together.

Spock scanned it with his tricorder. "No one aboard, Captain. The damage control measures are ingenious and effectual."

"So where is this alleged Free Agent?" McCoy asked. "Assuming the local fauna haven't invited him to dinner, as the main course."

He found himself getting worried. Hell of a place to lose a Free Agent of the Federation.

"Setting up a warning perimeter, possibly," Kirk speculated.

"No," said a voice from above and behind them, and McCoy felt the back of his neck tingle suddenly—from the bio-belt, or maybe only from the short hairs rising.

They whirled in one motion, eyes reaching to confirm the astonishment of the voice.

The woman uncoiled from the wide branch of one of the unit-trees which stretched out almost above their heads. She stood up and moved out on a narrower branch without effort or thought, and she was holding some sort of weapon on them. It looked like a coil of light which played through her hand—as if it could be rope, sword, spear. And deadly in her hands.

Apart from that, McCoy thought, she was possibly a gorgeous female. He was not certain of what species.

She was humanoid, certainly. She even looked, for all practical purposes, Human. But there was a hint of something almost feral about the tawny eyes. The matching tawny mane seemed to grow to some natural length and shape which she merely shook back. She moved on the branch with a curious certainty, as if she were of some hunting species as at home there as McCoy was on solid ground.

But there was also some shocking contrast of utter civility and star-spanning culture. She wore soft boots and a coppery bodysuit which looked as it if were poured out of the living metal, cut in lines of elegant simplicity which suggested that she was indifferent to fashion, but not to design. But more than that, there was some aura about her which struck McCoy as being like no woman he had ever seen, of any species. Possibly some part of it was merely the knowledge that she was a Free Agent of the Federation, and of what that had to cost and imply. But also there was a power of certainty about her which he had seen in few men, few beings of any sex or species—something like the bedrock certainty of a Spock, but with a glint of humor in the tawny eyes which was rather more like the sunlit ease of a Kirk. She looked at the three of them as if seeing were an enjoyment, as if she saw them fully and fearlessly, not merely how they looked, but what they *were*.

And the net result of her estimate of them was a pleasure which lit the clearing like morning.

McCoy supposed that she was beautiful. He was too busy looking at her to see. It didn't seem to be the important question.

He tried, with indifferent success, not to be surprised merely on the level that a Free Agent was a woman.

But there still was that surprise. This woman would be doing the toughest job in the known galaxy—going alone among enemies, putting herself into physical danger, and worse, into the moral danger of the kinds of decisions a Free Agent would make over the fate of worlds.

On the whole, McCoy might have picked a woman, if he had to pick anyone, for that job—but he would still have wanted to slay a few dragons for her. He saw a look on Kirk's face which suggested that McCoy would have company.

But this Free Agent looked quite prepared to do it herself, with or without the energy coil which played through her hand like a live thing, from a wrist projector.

Her eyes were without fear, but beyond the personal enjoyment which had brightened her face for a moment—something professional weighed the three men as if some decision were required. McCoy suddenly smelled trouble.

"We came to offer assistance," Kirk said. "I am Captain—"

"I know who you are, Captain Kirk," she said. "Or at least who you *were.*"

"*Were?*" Kirk asked, puzzled. "Forgive me, perhaps you have been out of touch. Permit me to present my First Officer—"

"I know Mr. Spock, too. Assuming that he still *is* Spock. And I know Doctor McCoy, by reputation."

McCoy bowed fractionally. He had seldom known a touch of Southern chivalry to do any harm. "I'm afraid you have the advantage of me, ma'am."

"Yes, I have." She did not smile.

"You have the advantage of all of us," Kirk said, "if you know of some reason why we might not be ourselves."

She nodded soberly. "Yes. I have that advantage, too. . . . Captain, in this sector forty-three known ships of many species, including Federation Starfleet crews, have abandoned the pattern and purpose of a lifetime. I am not fully certain why, nor of what they became. But I know that they became someone else. Or—*something* else."

"Then you know the fate of the missing ships?" Kirk asked.

"Partly." She cut off his unasked questions. "Not here. If you know because it has happened to you, there is no point. If not, there is no time."

She swung down from the tree, dropped lightly from half-again their height and landed without effort.

Kirk looked at her now on the level and found that she had to look up at him. Suddenly she looked to McCoy rather small and far too vulnerable to carry the job she had to carry. "How will you decide?" Kirk asked. "And by the same token, how will *we?* If something could change a starship crew and Captain, it could change anyone. What proof can we have that you are who, or what, we think?"

She shook her head. "None, Captain, on either side. I might point out that you have only me to thank for knowledge that the problem exists. But you already know that there is a mystery in the sector. I might have told you to disarm you."

Kirk nodded. "Well, we have dealt with identity and authenticity problems before. There is always the Vulcan mind-meld."

The tawny eyes approved the thought, but rejected it. "As what you believe I am, I could not consent to a mind-meld, even if I wanted to. As what I am, I would not."

"And what are you?" Kirk asked.

"I would prefer to tell you my name. I am—"

For the first time the Vulcan spoke—as if the words were wrenched out of him. "Sola Thane."

Kirk turned to look at the Vulcan.

"Sola Thane," Kirk said, "disappeared years ago."

Spock nodded. "Precisely."

Chapter 7

Kirk turned back to the woman, and now McCoy saw something new in the way he looked at her—as if all the fatigue had dropped away and something had clicked into place in the universe.

"Of course," Kirk said, with the tone of discovering a law of nature.

"*Of course?*" McCoy protested. "Spock jumps at a conclusion across a few light-years—and it seems obvious to *you?* Vulcan 'logic' must be contagious these days."

Spock looked as if he might for once have the grace to be embarrassed. "The inference was somewhat remote, but compelling, Doctor."

The woman smiled. "Indeed. I would be interested to hear *that* logic, Mr. Spock."

Spock faced her with some expression McCoy could not read. "I have made something of a study of your record."

Kirk turned to make his own study of the Vulcan.

"Sola Thane," Spock said, "was, among other things, the first non-Vulcan to participate with distinction in a Vulcan mental event which requires a high order of philosophical sophistication and pure logic."

"I suppose that's your department, Mr. Spock," Kirk said. "She also served with some distinction in Starfleet—including saving a starship in the *Endurance* incident." He turned to the woman almost accusingly. "If Mr. Spock is right—and I am sure that he is—you were slated to command a starship—when you resigned and disappeared."

She met Kirk's eyes. "I observe that you have made something of a study yourself, Captain Kirk. As I of you."

"Why did you give up your starship?" Kirk persisted.

"There was a question I had to solve. It required going back to my own roots."

"There was no record," Spock said, "of your planet of origin."

"No."

"It was Zaran," Spock said definitively.

It was not a question, but Sola Thane nodded. "We are both hybrids, Mr. Spock. We share your Human mother's world, which was my father's world."

"That explains it," McCoy muttered. He had been trying to place her look, her species. She *was* half-Human and looked almost wholly Human. But her other half was no more Human than Spock's Vulcan heritage—and it doubtless held as many surprises and pitfalls for them as mere Humans. The native species of Zaran was little known. It was supposed to have been a hunting species and was now kept in some form of subjugation by Humans who had fled Earth in the collapse of the old totalitarian empires. McCoy seemed to remember a couple of medical notes on the Zaran aboriginal species. He had not expected to meet a specimen here. "The females of your species," McCoy said, "didn't they have some special role in the hunt?"

"Doctor, they *were* the hunt." She looked at McCoy for a moment but did not pursue it. "Captain, we have very little time. This environment is hazardous. I have been broadcasting a signal which may discourage some predators, but its time is running out. I propose we adjourn to the *Enterprise*. If some mysterious effect has claimed you, it has done its job so thoroughly that I cannot detect the difference. And if it had claimed me, I believe you would be lost in any case. I require fast transport. Millions of lives and the survival of my species on Zaran depend on it."

Kirk looked at her carefully for a long moment. "Fast transport is *all* you require?"

"The rest I must do myself."

Kirk pulled out the command code message from the Chief of Staff and handed it to her without comment. A Free Agent would be able to read it. Or a Starship Captain. No one else.

But the tawny eyes read more than the message. "I see," she said. "Your ship has been placed at my disposal. I have not been entirely out of touch. Captain Kirk, you have become something of a legend. It is a legend of a ship which runs on loyalty to one man, and of a First Officer who serves only that man. All legends have their reason. It is unwise to tamper with them. I do require your ship for my purpose, but I require it with its working legend intact."

Kirk inclined his head fractionally. "My impulse would have been to cooperate fully with a Free Agent. The matter was not left to my impulse or judgment."

She nodded, seemed to come to a decision. "Captain, if you were less than you are, I would not tell you why the Chief of Staff would give me this authority. Your judgment is not in question. But you cannot know my mission. And my mission involves not only the fate of my species, but the fate of Starfleet. And, incidentally, of the Old Man himself. Possibly even the fate of intelligent life in the galaxy. My authority does not extend to telling you *how*."

Kirk was silent for a moment. "I thank you for telling me that much. I should warn you that I don't work well—blind."

She nodded. "Nor do I. But I cannot help you beyond that." She extended the card to him. "Let us agree, however, to endeavor not to reach the point which would make me use this over your resistance."

For the first time Kirk smiled fractionally, a little wryly. "I note you do not say that you will not."

"No."

His eyes took up the challenge. "All right. That's fair warning."

Her eyes laughed. "No. It is not. But perhaps you will not have to find out everything I should have warned you about."

Kirk smiled dangerously. "Then I won't warn you, either."

McCoy sighed, and if he had set words to that music, they would have been "Here we go again."

He turned to look for the expression of patient tolerance on Spock's face—and did not find it. The expression which *was* there McCoy could not read, or did not want to believe. Nor, McCoy suspected, could the Vulcan believe it himself. It was not even the prehistoric look McCoy had seen when Spock's reversion to the past in the ancient ice-caves of Sarpeidon had permitted Spock to want Zarabeth. It was much worse than that, and McCoy had the sudden sense that it was much more dangerous.

This was not the euphoria of the spores, nor the effect of some virus. This looked a lot like Spock, in his right mind, hit by some effect he himself had never experienced before in response to a woman.

McCoy looked back to Kirk and suddenly he knew that they were all in trouble. It was not even "Here we go again." It was some look McCoy had not seen since Kirk had found—and lost—Edith Keeler. Perhaps not even then. Edith had reached to summon the future out of the past where she had been born but never belonged. But this woman was at home in their present and in the stars—doing the one job which matched the danger, the scope, the moral hazard of a Starship Captain. Given Kirk, how could he not respond to that? And God help them all, how had McCoy never realized that there was bound to come a time when two men who had virtually become one would be one in this, too?

He saw Kirk turn to Spock, see the Vulcan's look, start to dismiss it as if he must have read it wrong, then look again and know that he read it exactly.

"Spock?" Kirk said almost involuntarily.

Spock visibly pulled himself together. "Nothing, Captain."

Kirk did not believe it, but he saw that Spock wanted badly to get back into his Vulcan suit. "Very well, Mr. Spock."

But the woman had caught it, too. "Mr. Spock," she said, "you also have become legend—on Vulcan and between the stars. I have long known of that legend and followed it with interest, and with a wish to discuss one or two points of philosophy and logic with you. But now I would like to know what caused you to study my record."

Spock looked at her stonily now, but did not attempt a denial. "In the legend about *you*—your behavior sounded . . . logical. That is not—common."

"In my sex?" she asked.

"In your species. At least—not in the one we share."

She laughed then, a low, clear chuckle. "And *did* you find my behavior logical, Mr. Spock? I would be most interested in your opinion."

"Yes," Spock said. "But you seemed to be *enjoying* it."

She laughed again. *"There,* Spock, is the point of philosophy I wanted to discuss with you."

"Not here," Spock said. "I have permitted myself to become illogically distracted. We should not have remained here."

"Now we can go," Sola agreed. She turned toward her scoutship. "Beam up. I will need the scout."

But then McCoy saw her whirl, crouching, even before his bio-belt gave warning—as if her senses were built into her own skin.

Some animal leaped out from the sheltering flank of the scoutship.

It resembled no Earth animal, but the jumbled impression which came through to McCoy was of something like a saber-toothed wolfhound—as tall as a man, and faster.

It leaped for Sola Thane's throat . . .

Chapter 8

Spock saw the coil of light flash out from Sola Thane's hand, circling the animal's throat, stunning it and bringing it down at her feet.

Spock's phaser was in his hand, but he had not been quick enough to fire before she had struck.

"There is a pack," she said as calmly as a Vulcan might have.

But Spock and Kirk were already moving, as if choreographed, to stand at her shoulders and cover her back. And McCoy moved in, fast, to form a hollow square.

"Beam up," Spock said, reaching for his communicator. But the clearing erupted animals. They were faster than *snarth* and could cover a hundred meters while a hunter thought about it.

But Sola Thane's coil of light was there to meet them, its tip flipping from one to another by some dynamic of skill which Spock did not understand but was forced to commend as a fighting skill to equal any he had seen. He saw no fear in her, merely an intent concentration—somewhat superior to his own at the moment.

He focused on dropping animals. And on keeping an eye on Kirk. The Human was not up to his usual standard and this sudden stress could drain him, cause him to make a wrong move. Spock noted that he was trusting Sola with part of the job of guarding Kirk's back, as if he could trust both her logic and her commitment. But though her logic and her light coil were used faultlessly, it was not enough. Animals fell, stunned—but not soon enough. Momentum carried the great beasts, even unconscious, to crash at the fighting party's feet, or through it.

Spock pulled Kirk out of the way of one, Sola deflected another. A third caromed off McCoy's shoulder, knocking him half-senseless until Sola steadied him.

Kirk was fighting and dodging with most of his usual agility, but Spock knew that the Human was burning his last reserves and could not keep it up.

Spock reached his communicator, but it was knocked out of his hand as an animal hit him squarely. It was an impact which would have broken Human bones. Spock was jarred. He was still rolling up from the fall when two animals broke from the cover of the scoutship and leaped for Kirk's throat.

Sola dropped one out of the air, but the other was past her and at Kirk's throat. Kirk got an arm up, and the animal's teeth closed on the arm, not the throat. But twice Kirk's weight jerked at the arm and hit him, at express speed, bearing him down. He fell, hard, and was out.

Sola's light-line coiled around the animal's throat, knocking it out and pulling it off, and Spock poured a phaser stun into it when it was clear of Kirk.

But Kirk did not move and Spock saw the white-to-the-bone look of deep shock in the Human's face. Spock dropped to one knee beside the Human's body and his left hand clamped a pressure point to stop the bleeding from the arm. He fired across the body as the animals kept coming.

Sola fought her way toward Spock, foot by foot, until she

stood beside him. Her free hand dropped to touch his temple and he felt the flow of some kind of mental contact which was alien to him, something which struck him as born of jungles and of ancestors even more fierce than his own Vulcan breed. It cut right through the shield he had set up, and he knew it would undermine his defenses, perhaps fatally. But he sensed her purpose was to save Kirk, and he could not deny her.

Then the mental touch seemed to gather amplifying force from him and to flow out through her in some great and terrible mental warning—the psionic hunting cry of the most formidable species on its planet.

Spock saw the charging animals pull up or veer off, confused, and in some dim recess of their rudimentary brains—terrified.

One crashed into McCoy again at the last second, and Spock saw him again get hit on the already damaged shoulder and knocked out.

"The scoutship," Sola ordered in the tone of command, and Spock was giving no argument. It would take the *Enterprise* longer to hear them and beam them up than they had.

He picked Kirk up in one arm and was not surprised to see Sola get an arm around McCoy and move him bodily toward the double doors of the scout.

The animals were losing their terror, starting to move in again. The scout's double-doors opened to Sola Thane's voice, and she heaved McCoy in and turned to cover Spock as he stepped up with Kirk. She dropped an animal as she jumped in after him. The doors closed on the muzzle of another great beast, then recoiled like turbolift safety doors, threatening to let it in. Sola snapped the last of her weapon's charge straight into its face and it fell back. The doors closed with finality.

The scoutship began to shake with the impact of animals still crashing into it in their fury. As a rule, they could not have damaged it, but Spock was dubious of the recent repairs.

Sola bent swiftly to check McCoy and appropriated his medical kit. "The doctor is unconscious, an arm dislocated, but in no danger," she said. She turned to Kirk, running McCoy's medical scanner with precision.

"He has been suffering from old injuries and cumulative

stress," Spock said flatly, "and I believe that a Oneness has made persistent efforts to absorb him, with some momentary successes. He is in great danger."

She read the results on the scanner, and Spock saw her face, under the tawny look, go white. It told him all he needed to know, about both of them.

"Mr. Spock," she said. "I assume you can fly this antique. I have had some medical training as a Free Agent."

Spock merely nodded. If it flew, he could fly it. A Free Agent had the field-medical skills of a doctor. At her gesture he yielded Kirk into her care, putting him down on a narrow bunk while she knelt beside it and replaced Spock's pressure-hold with her own.

Spock stood up and looked down at Kirk's bone-white face for a moment, but what he saw was the shape of a long emptiness if the last of that living color and presence ran out.

He went forward, and his eyes and hands methodically read the controls of the obsolete Starfleet-type scout—possibly one of the small Federation ships which had vanished in the Marie Celeste sector. He could have flown it, blind—which was virtually the case. He no longer tried to disguise from himself that the mental assault from the Oneness and his unsuccessful efforts to shelter Kirk from it had eroded his own mental defenses against the one thing he feared most. And the woman had completed his undoing. He felt a dark rebellion against his fate, a fate which she had sealed. But then again, perhaps he had already been too far down that road to save himself. There was nowhere to go and no one to go to. Vulcan was weeks away at maximum warp. Humans were far too fragile, even if he would, or could—

Spock fired the impulse-power engines and lifted the ship slowly out of the clearing, careful not so much of the jury-rigged repairs but of Kirk's life hanging on a thread which might snap at any sudden acceleration or stress.

Spock flew the scoutship as if its cargo were infinitely fragile and infinitely precious.

He saw his hands locked whitely onto the controls, and Spock of Vulcan knew that the non-emotion disciplines were finally crumbling entirely, and that that was his death sentence.

Chapter 9

Kirk's consciousness seemed to float somewhere above his body, as if he could look down and see competent, swift hands bind up his bleeding arm, press a spray hypo home, then hold a pressure-point again as even the dressing did not fully stop the bleeding.

All of that seemed to have nothing to do with him.

He was vastly remote from it all, unconcerned.

It came to him rather quietly that this fit the descriptions of the death experience. Somewhere he rebelled against that, but even the rebellion remained remote, and he knew he did not give it the vital force he would have given it—*had* given it, many times. Once too often, possibly.

"The animal's fangs injected some systemic poison," the woman's voice said. "I've given him everything I could

against the poison and shock, but in his weakened condition
—it could kill him."

"*We* have killed him," Spock's voice said. "Emotions have
killed him. We knew the danger. We stood there talking like
children. I do not exempt myself. Least of all myself."

"And me," she said, not evading the tone of accusation.

"Yes." The Vulcan spoke in a tone of barely leashed
ferocity.

"It is not logic to ignore what is real, Mr. Spock. Including
emotions. But it is true that I miscalculated, seriously."

"How?"

"I had thought you would still be locked into your Vulcan
pattern."

"Hope that I *am*. And that he does not die."

"It is too late for you, Mr. Spock. If he lives, you will have
to acknowledge what it means to you that I exist."

"It can mean nothing," Spock said harshly. "Not if he dies.
And not if he lives. In either case, I am a dea—" The
Vulcan's voice broke off. "I am—a Vulcan," he amended,
but Kirk still felt that he heard the Vulcan's voice saying "I
am a dead man."

Kirk felt himself jerked back toward his body as if his soul
were on a string. Once, on Vulcan, when Spock had thought
Kirk was dead, Kirk knew that the Vulcan had answered
T'Pau's "Live long and prosper, Spock," with "I shall do
neither, for I have killed my Captain, and my friend." That
knowledge had pulled Kirk through a tough one once or
twice. But what could the Vulcan mean now—that he was
dead even if Kirk lived? Something to do with Sola? From
some strange perspective Kirk could look down to see
Spock's hands go white on the controls. But the Vulcan's face
was drawn and faintly flushed, as if with some fever.

"He will not die, Spock," Sola said. "And—neither will
you."

"What do you count on to save him?" Spock asked. "That
he saw you? That he—loved you?"

"Partly," she said. "But chiefly, that he knew *you* saw me.
I do not think he would miss that. Nor leave you now. He
would rise from the dead, if necessary. Which it may be . . ."

She bent over Kirk then and took his face between her
hands. "I do not give you permission to go. No one here gives
you permission."

He knew already that he could not go. For the white hands on the controls, if nothing else, he could not go. But there *was* else: the hands which held his face, and a universe which could still deliver such a surprise package . . .

He had been tired for a moment. That was all.

He felt a kind of rushing sensation, and once more his consciousness seemed to be at home in the body. There was pain now, but also he could feel the touch of Sola's hands as if a current flowed from them.

He opened his eyes and looked up into her face. He could hold to consciousness only for a moment, but he saw that she knew he had come back, and from how far.

Then he drifted down into ordinary darkness, but from somewhere he thought he heard Sola say, "He will live, Spock. And you will have no excuse not to deal with what I am."

"What you are—is *his*."

"Spock, I may be the only non-Vulcan who would know why it will take more than words to save you. There is only one act which will."

Spock spoke then in the tone of murder. "Do not presume to pity me!"

"Never, Spock. But I do not give you permission to go, either."

Kirk tried fitfully to stir, alarm bells going off in his head. It was always a mistake to think of the Vulcan as if he were Human. He was *not*. What deadly Vulcanism did Sola and Spock know about, which Kirk did not? Something which was triggered by what Spock could not deny he had felt for Sola? And something which Spock could not have, because he counted her as belonging to Kirk . . . ?

Abruptly Kirk knew that he had seen Spock's stressed, fevered look before, long ago on Vulcan. It was the *pon farr*—the time of mating, the madness which Spock had dreaded and hoped to be spared.

Kirk fought for consciousness, but he could not make it. And would she know what she had to do . . . ?

McCoy stirred and opened his eyes. His own pain was blinding, but he held the dislocated arm to his side and hitched himself over to where Sola worked over Kirk. He read the settings she had used on the spray hypo and looked at her with a new professional respect. But when he ran the scanner over Kirk, he scowled. "He's hanging by a thread," he said under his breath to Sola. But Spock heard. McCoy saw the look on his face and wished he had kept his mouth shut.

In moments Spock was signaling the *Enterprise* and matching velocity to settle them into the landing bay.

"Full medical team to the landing bay," Spock ordered. "The Captain's condition is critical."

Then they were in and the landing deck was pressurizing around them. The moment it was pressurized, Chapel, M'Benga, and a medical team were swarming toward the scoutship, guiding null-grav stretchers.

But Spock turned from the controls without a word and came and took Kirk up in his arms. Sola surrendered him without comment, but kept her hand on her pressure-hold which was still stopping the bleeding.

McCoy thought that the look in the Vulcan's eyes warned of some dangerous Vulcan state. Spock carried Kirk out into the landing bay and walked through the medical team without pause.

McCoy signaled the stretchers aside. It was quicker, even easier, to use the Vulcan's strength and move Kirk directly to Sickbay. And there was something to be said for being carried by a living presence rather than a grav-stretcher. Especially if it was by the Vulcan, who had carried his Captain off of more than one battlefield. That presence and the touch of Sola's hand might well register with Kirk wherever he was, and keep him somewhere within reach of coming back.

Chapel inspected McCoy's dangling right arm as they moved to the turbolift. "What do you think you're doing moving around with that, Doctor?" she asked.

McCoy shook his head. "That's the least of my worries."

In the turbolift Chapel shot McCoy's shoulder joint full of neo-procaine and the pain eased. But McCoy would not take time to have the dislocated arm put back in place.

They were arriving at Sickbay. Spock put Kirk down carefully on the main diagnostic table. The life-sign readouts were shockingly low. At McCoy's signal Dr. M'Benga brought an instant IV to replace blood. Chapel moved in with a pressure clip to replace Sola's hold.

Sola had to pry her fingers loose, McCoy saw, and did so,

not paying attention to it. McCoy reached over and caught her left hand with his. "Muscle spasms," he said. "You must have been holding on to him as if your life depended on it."

She looked up quietly and nodded. "That's right, Doctor."

The Vulcan stood by without expression, looking down at Kirk.

Then Sola turned to Kirk, and while Chapel and McCoy checked the readouts, the Zaran seemed to do her own evaluation—or perhaps treatment. She put a hand on Kirk's forehead, on his temples, on the injured arm.

It was Chapel who pointed out that where Sola touched him there was electrical activity registering on some of the instruments. "Like the old Kirlian patterns," Christine Chapel said to McCoy, "which were said to show results of psychic healing."

"What *are* you?" McCoy asked Sola.

"A female of my species," she said. "Unfortunately an unbonded one. Therefore of erratic powers. But it should be of some help."

"Psychic healing?"

Sola shook her head. "Not precisely. It is a Zaran psionic technology for the transfer of life-energy."

She stood then at Kirk's head, letting her hands rest on his temples, and McCoy could almost see the life-energy flowing out of her and into Kirk. McCoy saw no harm in it. There was not much harm anyone could do him, now. The vital signs showed that Kirk was dying.

Then even the instruments began to agree. The computer display showed a flow of warmth, energy, circulation. McCoy saw Christine Chapel's eyes riveted to the computer readouts. "Vital signs improving, Doctor," she said.

McCoy saw Spock's face, the Vulcan control eroded almost completely. "He is still critical, Spock," McCoy said. "But she's giving him a chance."

"*Still* critical?" Spock asked. He scanned the life signs. "There is," he conceded, "visible improvement."

McCoy nodded. "I'm saying it's still touch and go. The cumulative stress—and some kind of pretty virulent poison. But you know him, Spock. He'll fight."

"With what, Doctor?" Spock asked with what sounded like bitterness. "How many times?"

Sola swayed fractionally, and McCoy saw that her face was

drained. He moved toward her. "You have to stop now," he said.

But she shook her head microscopically and continued, going suddenly white to the bone. Then Spock stepped behind her and put one hand on her shoulder, one into the mane of tawny hair, the long Vulcan fingers seeking contact points known to Spock's own psionic technology. "Let her continue," Spock said. He seemed to make some massive effort, and McCoy had the sudden feeling that it was at the expense of the last of his mental reserves or controls.

McCoy started to protest, but there was a new flow of life-force to Kirk, as if she could draw it from the Vulcan and pass it on.

The Vulcan must have divined that it would work, and it did.

They kept at it until Spock also looked drained white, and McCoy feared for the Vulcan, whom they all tended to think of as indestructible. He was not, as McCoy very well knew, and he knew that Spock would drain the last drop of his own life-force for this.

But Kirk's vital signs were beginning to move toward the low normal range, and his face even had a touch of color. On McCoy's signal Chapel had given Kirk another powerful detoxicant against the poison and sealed up the bleeding arm. It would have to do.

McCoy moved in and took one of Sola's hands where it touched Kirk's temples. He could almost feel the flow of something himself—a tingle in his hand. "That's enough. Stop now."

Slowly she opened her eyes and focused on McCoy.

"You've done the job," McCoy said. "Stop before I have two more patients."

She started to look over her shoulder at Spock, but the movement overstrained some precariously maintained balance, and she swayed. Spock held her and reached down himself to pull her hands away. Finally she let go.

After a moment she straightened and took her own weight, then turned to face Spock. "Thank you, Mr. Spock."

Spock shook his head. "Necessary." He still looked at her stonily.

"Spock," McCoy protested, "she almost certainly saved his life."

Spock turned to him bleakly. "She was the cause of his danger. As *I* was."

"Those overgrown werewolves were the cause of his danger, Spock," McCoy said impatiently. "Not to mention a few kinds of hell he's been through lately. And what did she—or *you*—do? Take a few seconds to deal with the unprecedented?"

"With emotions, Doctor. *Mine,*" Spock said.

Abruptly McCoy felt his medical alarms going off. When the Platonians had tortured and humiliated Kirk, Spock had actually admitted to emotions for the first time, but only to insist that "You must express your emotions—and I must master *mine.*" Over the years Spock had perhaps lost that battle in certain crucial respects, but he had never surrendered.

But now what kind of Vulcanism would it touch off if Spock could neither master nor deny what McCoy had seen in the clearing? And what was Spock supposed to do about it if he had also seen what Kirk felt? Just when you thought you had Spock figured, there would be some Vulcan booby trap opening under all their feet—swift, and probably lethal.

"Mr. Spock, I want to examine you," McCoy said.

"Doctor," the Vulcan snapped, "you will not pull medical rank on me now. I suffer from no condition which you could detect or correct."

"Do you suffer from a condition which I could *not* detect or correct?" McCoy demanded.

"Physician," Spock said, "heal thyself. *I* have duties." He turned on a heel and stepped to the intercom. "Bridge. Maintain survey orbit. Assume attempt at concealment of starship trap. Maintain increased security on the ship. Spock out."

McCoy was about to start in again when he felt Sola attach herself to his injured shoulder. The agony had come back. Before he could protest a further draining of her power, she slipped a hand under his armpit, and by some swift move of strength and precision, she slipped the bone back into its socket. There was a moment of blinding pain—and then under her hands the pain left as if it had never been—and he felt healed in more than the shoulder. McCoy looked at her incredulously. "Who's the doctor around here?" he complained.

She smiled. "You are, Doctor. That is merely the trail skill of a huntress."

"Or a miracle," McCoy muttered.

But Spock cut him off. "Will the Captain die?" he asked Sola.

She turned and met Spock's eyes. "No. Not again."

"Come with me," Spock ordered.

Her eyes seemed to take up some challenge. "Yes, Mr. Spock," she said, and turned to obey.

Chapter 10

Sola Thane matched the Vulcan's stride through the corridors of the *Enterprise*, and she was perhaps the only female aboard who could have matched his pace. He was an aimed bullet. Certainly she was the only being aboard who could meet his strength in what was to come. Humans were far too fragile. She recoiled from the thought of what his strength, unleashed, in his present state, would do to fragile Human flesh. She wanted to back away from what it would do to her own.

Worse, she knew that what the Humans would have called her heart was not here. It was back in Sickbay with the man who had won a still-fragile victory over death—perhaps for *her*. She wanted nothing more than to go to him. But she had wanted nothing more than that for years.

It had not been possible. She was not Human, at least not
in those vital respects which could make her a danger to him
unless she won her own fight. Strictly speaking, it was not
possible now. But she had felt her years-long resolve to stay
away from him crumble when she faced him in the clearing. If
the chemistry she had long expected had not materialized,
they could have backed away. As it was, he would not back
off. Nor would she.

Except that what neither of them had expected was Spock.
That had been an error in her own philosophy.

She looked at him now, hard, taut, angry with her for the
danger she had allowed to Kirk and for the death sentence
she had sealed for Spock himself. She was probably the only
non-Vulcan in the galaxy who could understand that completely. Her training on Vulcan and her need for help with
her own powers had led her finally to a link with T'Pau of
Vulcan.

Spock reached a door and stepped into the field to open
it for her. She stepped through, the moment when she
met his eyes stressing that she did not hesitate. The turbolift had deposited them in officers' country. The door
opened on Vulcan—a red weapon wall, a demonic looking
flame-idol.

He engaged the privacy lock, not offering explanation. He
had brought her to his quarters. She wondered whether he
had already reached the stage where the life force took over
in a last effort to save his life and he would not be able to
control his actions—or even to remember them. If so, things
would move very quickly. And she found that she was not
prepared.

"Free Agent Thane," he said in the strained tone of
cracking discipline, "you are of command rank and the ship
has been placed at your disposal. You will now assume
command and have me locked away."

"No, Mr. Spock," she said. "I will not."

"You have no alternative. I cannot be responsible for my
actions. I will not explain, and an explanation would be
unavailing. Lock me away. It is my right."

"No, Spock. It is *not*. You have an obligation—to the man
whose life we just fought for."

"Yes," he said grimly. "I do." He said it as a sentence of
doom.

"To die nobly?" She shook her head fiercely. "It is not going to be that way, Spock."

"You do not understand."

"On the contrary, I do. I did not study on Vulcan for nothing. Yours is perhaps the only free species which shares some of my Zaran half's ferocity and powers. But we do not try to suppress emotion to the point where it must explode— fatally. What you do not wish to tell me is that your mating bond was challenged and broken, and you have spent years attempting to get out of that box, before your control broke and sent you amok on a ship of Humans."

He looked as if she had hit him. She had read the secret he had defended even from Kirk. And she knew that she had to hammer through the rest of his defenses while he was still vulnerable, and still in control. "What did you plan to do, Spock—if it hit you between the stars? Perhaps it would hit when you were alone with one or two Humans, then what? Lock yourself away? But you would break any lock when control broke. What would you do then?"

Spock looked at her without flinching. "Die," he said.

She nodded. "It's not going to be that easy, Spock."

"Free Agent Thane, there exists on this ship a powerful collective mind which was already eroding mental barriers— mine, his, doubtless others. For a Vulcan the link between mind and body is strong. Under normal circumstances perhaps I would have retained the capacity to resist. My circumstances have not been normal for some time. I do not expect or require that you understand."

"You went home to Vulcan," she divined, "and tried to pay the price of Kolinahr—of total non-emotion—for the safety of the Humans who had come to mean too much to you."

His eyes narrowed and she saw the fever flare in them. "Do not understand me too well," he warned.

She did not back off. "You knew there would come a day when Uhura or Christine Chapel or someone else would pay a price to save your life. How could anyone who knew your value, who loved you, not save you? But the price paid would be too high. So you went. But there was a catch in that theory, too, Spock. If you loved them enough to leave them and to lock yourself into the straightjacket of Kolinahr, then any claim to non-emotion you ever had was a fraud and Kolinahr was forever beyond your reach."

His eyes were lethal now. "I do not require you to give me a lesson in philosophy."

"Spock, I *am* a lesson in philosophy. I am possibly the only lesson you still needed to learn. That was what your body knew in the clearing. That is what it knows now. And that is what will kill you if you do not finally break out of that box."

He moved suddenly and she thought he would take her throat in his hands. But he lifted her chin with one hand, not gently, his fingers biting into her. "Do not patronize me. Do you wish me to admit that I see you match my logic without giving up emotion? Very well. I see it. Do you wish me to admit that you were the straw which broke a Vulcan's back? I admit it. I am far beyond the point where admissions can harm me—or help me. I require nothing of you, except that you leave now and set an interlock I cannot break. Go!"

She shook her head.

His hand tightened on her face, making her realize that his steel strength could break bones, even hers. "I have already lost physiological control in one significant respect," he grated. "Go *now!*"

She did not move. "I said it would take more than words to save you, Spock. There is only one thing which will. We both know that I am not going."

Through his hand she felt him caught by a sudden uncontrollable shudder. She knew that some deep part of him fought for the life she offered. But he shook his head. "Even if I would and you would—we could not. You do not belong to me. You belong to him. We both know that you always have. No. He is my friend."

She let her own temper flare. "Whereas your death of course will solve his problem!" Her tone was fierce now and she let him see that she would fight for his life, even against *him*. "And of course it will solve *mine*," she continued scathingly. "I will go to him over your dead body, and we will live happily ever after!"

Her hunting blood was up and she could see that his blood burned. His eyes were flame. His grip tightened on her and then flung her back as if in a last effort to save both of them.

"Fine," she said. "You have given him a taste of unity—and withdrawn it. Die now and you will drive him into the arms of Oneness. He will have nowhere else to go. But spare yourself, Mr. Spock. Don't bother to fight for your life.

Or—your love. It is much easier to crawl off into your own old pattern and die than to break out of all boxes and live."

He took a step toward her as if he would break her neck. Suddenly she did not care if he tried. And she knew that she had succeeded not only in rousing him to fight her. She had summoned her own Zaran half to meet him, as she had intended. She lived in her Human half a good deal around Humans. But the Zaran in her was neither safe nor civil. It did not, in hot blood, know the meaning of fear—although she knew fear still as a kind of swift undercurrent which was almost a pleasure. Here was jungle to match her jungle, the desert-bred Vulcan who would match wit and muscle against a *le matya* the size of *Tyrannosaurus Rex*. He was entitled to the ferocity of his passion. And her Zaran was entitled to the ferocity of her own. Her Zaran did not so much love the sunlit wholeness of Kirk which another part of her worshipped. Her Zaran was drawn to the ragged and monumental effort at wholeness which was Spock. She had seen it in the clearing and known that life would never be simple again. If there was an error in his philosophy, and there was, it was a giant error, possible only to a giant. And she must be making an error of a similar size—because she knew now that it was not for his sake, nor even for Kirk's that she would take him on. It was for herself . . .

He stopped himself and his voice was so harsh and shaken that it came out barely above a whisper. "I would not choose to die—*now*. I am Vulcan enough to have no choice."

"You are more than Vulcan. You are *Spock*. You have a choice. And *I* have one. I have made it."

"You made your choice in the clearing."

"That was a choice I had made long ago—before I knew how much you were Spock."

She moved toward him slowly, deliberately, letting her eyes tell him that she had no pity for him and no mercy. She knew it would have been easier for him in many ways to be allowed to crawl off and die in the dignity of his own custom, even if it meant the agony of *pon farr*.

"I will not permit you the luxury of dying, Spock," she said aloud, moving almost to touch him with her body. She could feel the heat of his.

He raised a hand as if to strike her. "I do not require or accept any charity!"

She lifted her head. "*I* do not give any."

He locked her arms behind her and pulled her against him, and for a moment he thought he would break her with his strength. She did not break, nor flinch. He started to break away from her and found that he could not, would not.

Spock of Vulcan felt the world dissolve in flame.

Chapter 11

McCoy left Chapel to watch Kirk and went to the bio-comps. Kirk was, technically, holding his own. But there was some look about him which McCoy did not like, as if he were the battlefield of some conflict of forces.

McCoy had tried to rouse him and could not.

McCoy wanted Spock—possibly the Vulcan should even try the mind-meld, although God knew what effect that would have now.

What worried McCoy was that the Vulcan wasn't in Sickbay. As a rule you couldn't move him out with a tractor beam—short of some life-or-death crisis.

And maybe that was what it *was*.

The bio-comps would have nothing on this for Vulcans which McCoy did not already know.

McCoy set a scan for all known medical, biological and related information on Zarans.

ZARAN NATIVE SPECIES. ORIGINAL CULTURE NOW OBSCURED BY TERRAN-HUMAN INFILTRATION AND CONQUEST FROM LONG-JUMP SHIP ESCAPING COLLAPSE OF OLD EARTH TOTALI-TARIAN EMPIRES.

NATIVE ZARAN CULTURE BELIEVED ONLY EXAMPLE OF HUNT-ING CULTURE RAISED TO HIGH LEVEL. EXTREMELY HAZARDOUS PLANET, UNSUITED TO AGRICULTURE BUT WITH PLENTIFUL GAME AND EXCEPTIONALLY HAZARDOUS PREDATORS, DEVEL-OPED A STRONG, HIGHLY ADAPTABLE SPECIES ATTUNED TO THE HUNT AS SCIENCE, ART, AND BASIS OF SOCIAL ORDER AND MATING CUSTOM.

AS IN SOME FELINES—E.G., ANDORIAN GRAYTH, TERRAN LIONS, ETC.—THE FEMALES ARE THE PRIMARY HUNTRESSES.

ZARAN FEMALES APPEAR TO HAVE CERTAIN EMPATHIC AND PSIONIC POWERS USED IN THE HUNT, IN HEALING, AND IN MATING. CERTAIN ZARAN FEMALES, WHEN BONDED TO A LIFE-MATE MALE, APPEAR CAPABLE OF JOINING A HUNTING BAND INTO ONE PSIONIC UNITY.

ONE HEREDITARY STRAIN OF SUCH FEMALES APPEARED TO BE DEVELOPING THE CAPACITY TO JOIN LARGER AND LARGER UNITS, FOR LONGER PERIODS. THE LAST OF THIS LINE, ZOLAN-THA, FIRST WELCOMED, THEN LED THE RESISTANCE AGAINST THE HUMAN FORCE WHICH CALLED ITSELF THE TOTALITY. HER FATE REMAINS UNKNOWN. IT IS RUMORED THAT SHE HAD A FEMALE CHILD, PERHAPS BY A HUMAN FATHER. IT IS NOT KNOWN WHETHER SUCH A HYBRID WOULD BE VIABLE. . . .

"Want to bet?" McCoy muttered. Before he could go on, there was a crash against his door, and he turned to see Mr. Dobius stagger through it.

The giant Tanian moved like a puppet controlled by two masters—lurching one way and then another. Finally he stopped, paralyzed—and dropped as if poleaxed.

McCoy was in time to catch the seven-foot Tanian as he collapsed. It was something of an embarrassment of riches. McCoy finally got him lowered into a chair and was able to swear quietly over a new wrench to his injured shoulder while he ran a scanner over the Tanian.

There was no apparent injury or sickness, but there was some peculiar mental pattern. The Tenian was something of an anomaly in any case. The bifurcated head actually housed what amounted to two brains, each of which could, at need, control the body.

McCoy played a hunch and put a brain scan on the analyzer. It showed an odd pattern in the right brain half, and something different but equally odd in the left. Then McCoy ran a test pattern he had taken himself on Gailbraith's One.

McCoy swore then, less quietly.

The right brain pattern matched Gailbraith's One.

"McCoy to Bridge," he said into the intercom. "Mr. Spock to Sickbay."

Uhura's voice came back. "Mr. Spock hasn't been to the Bridge since you returned from the planet, Doctor. May I help you?"

I doubt it, McCoy thought. *I'm going to need a lot more help than that.*

"No, thank you, Uhura," he said. "I'll find him."

But it was some time before he could be sure that the Tanian was in no immediate danger—and that nothing could rouse him.

He called Dr. M'Benga and an orderly to take Dobius to a treatment room, and he headed for Spock's quarters, feeling the urgency of needing to report this to the Vulcan.

But he had somehow sensed it would have been a worse mistake to have Uhura locate Spock at that moment . . .

Chapter 12

Spock watched Sola emerge from the lounge fresher. The fabricators had provided clothing to replace the coppery bodysuit.

She had programmed a simple close-fitting coverall, almost absurdly demure, zipped to the throat and plain enough for a nunnery—except that the fabric was meant to be felt with the fingertips, and any abbot would have admitted her at his peril. . . .

Spock found that he took some satisfaction in every privacy the outfit afforded, and every inch which would remain—the phrase came unbidden—for his eyes only.

Perhaps she saw the look. She came and stood close to him, not touching him, her eyes reading him as if to see whether she had bought life, or merely time.

He was not certain. Somewhere he felt his need to possess her threatening to close down on his heart again. But for the moment he could breathe.

"I shall be in Sickbay," he said.

She shook her head. "It is for me to go."

"Better if he does not see you now. When he is strong enough, I will answer for what I permitted myself. Now he is fighting for more than his life."

"His love?" she asked.

"Wasn't that what you counted on to save him?" Spock heard the harshness in his voice and knew that it was for himself. "Wasn't that what you promised him?"

She lifted her head and met his eyes. "Spock, that is a promise I will still keep, if he will let me."

Spock looked at her in simple astonishment. Whatever he had expected, it was not that. "How?" he asked.

She reached out to touch him. "Spock, I do not know how I will walk out of this door now. But I will, and you will let me."

"Will I?"

She smiled ruefully. "Right now I wish you would not. But I knew that risk. Spock, could you value him less because you have known me?"

"No."

"Then could I value *him* less?"

After a moment he said, "No."

"I do not know where it will lead, Spock, but I will not pretend that either of you does not exist."

He felt again the stirring of something which was not logic. *"Go,* then. You should have locked me away. If you were going to go to him, by what right do you bring him *this?"*

Her eyes flared. "What right did I need? Should I have brought him your dead body?"

"If that was your only reason . . ." he began harshly. Then his own sense of justice stopped him. "If that was your reason, it was sufficient. My life is yours. Do not concern yourself with it or me again. Go."

"Stubborn Vulcan," she said. "I would have done it for that. Are you too blind to see that I *did* not? Or that I cannot move to go?"

For the first time he saw her falter.

He pulled her to him then, and for a long moment she

allowed herself to rest against his strength. Then she straightened. "Send me to him, Spock. I have no power to go." Then she shook her head. "That is not true, either, Spock. I do. And I will."

She started to turn. He stopped her with a touch. "Go as you were in the moment you saw him. My weakness cannot be an argument against his strength."

"No," she said, "but your *strength* can."

She looked at him as if the sight would have to last her forever. Then she turned and did not look back.

"Sola," he said as she reached the door. He had not used the name, not any name.

She turned and saw that he had merely wanted to say it. Her tawny eyes laughed then, and he saw that some effort had dropped away from her.

"Spock," she said, and went out.

He stayed for a moment attempting to recapture the disciplines of Vulcan, without entire success. He was not certain whether he was guilty of treason, or of loyalty. But he lived, and he knew that the man who was fighting his solitary battle in Sickbay would not be left to fight it alone.

Then with the return of clarity Spock realized that something had been nagging at him somewhere below the level of logic, on that level which the Human would have called intuition.

Was it not exceedingly convenient that they had arrived at the mathematical center of nowhere to find a Free Agent of the Federation—and the one woman in the galaxy who could have been expected to have this effect on Captain James T. Kirk? Not to mention on— But perhaps that effect on Spock had *not* been expected.

Was there someone who could have predicted from the record at least the first effect? Someone who could have arranged their rendezvous with the inevitable? Someone who could have arranged to have the *Enterprise* come here?

There were at least two logical answers to that. He liked neither of them.

Spock stepped to the intercom. "Spock to Bridge. Check the status of the isolation-locks confining Ambassador Gailbraith and party."

Uhura's voice came back. "Mr. Spock, I was about to trace you. Doctor McCoy called urgently but left no message. Sir,

we are running computer checks which indicate that warning
sensors have been shut off throughout the ship—including
some to the isolation-locks. We can no longer verify that the
Ambassador's party has been isolated."

"Post guards," Spock said immediately.

"I have, sir. But, sir—those locks could not have been
opened, nor the sensors disconnected—from the *inside*."

"Precisely," Spock said. "Condition Seven. Assume that
one or more *Enterprise* personnel are, or may be, under alien
mental control."

"Sir, Condition Seven requires me to assume even that *you*
are, or may be."

"That is correct. Proceed on that assumption. Spock out."

In fact, Condition Seven required him to assume the same
of Uhura and all others, and not to discount the possibility
that he himself was affected without his knowledge.

In fact, he might have been one of two prime targets, and
the one most closely exposed . . .

Gailbraith was one possible answer to who might have
predicted and arranged. There was, in logic, a possible
answer which Spock liked still less: Sola Thane.

Spock was already moving out the door on the run.

Chapter 13

Kirk was alone in some far place. But it was a place where aloneness did not exist. He had only to stop fighting, let go, and he would not have to be locked back into his single skull, his stubbornly solitary body. It would be a relief. And it would clear the way for something else which he knew he had to stand aside and allow. He knew nothing very clearly, but he knew that there was some time-bomb ticking away for the Vulcan, and that Sola held some answer to that. He would have given anything if she did not. Except the one thing it would cost: Spock's life.

He struggled toward consciousness, aware of some desperate urgency to reach them. But he was dragged back down toward the Oneness. There was an illusion of safety there, a presence which had saved him once—and let him go . . . gray eyes and

*an ironic mouth and a quality of certainty which had warned
him that he would find what he needed—on the planet where he
had found her . . . And how would the gray eyes have known
that? Kirk was struggling for some vague memory of that
gray-eyed presence. It had held him in its power, saved him
from something, and—temporarily—let him go. But the compelling invitation was still there.*

*Then abruptly he was caught by another rip-tide, another
call to a different Oneness—this one a totality so strange that he
recoiled, knowing that it was utterly alien to him, and utterly
dangerous. It reached for him with a power which was
unanswerable. It was a call of Sirens, Sirens not of body but of
mind, Sirens of the Unknown— And he had always been the
Ulysses who would have had himself lashed to the mast to be
able to hear the Sirens' call . . .*

*But he was lashed to no safety now, and the Sirens of
Totality were claiming him . . .*

Kirk seemed to feel someone take his hand. He seized that
someone's hand as a life-line, crushing it, but it did not crush.
He pulled himself back, knowing that he had come very close
to both death and Oneness.

For a long time he merely looked at it and held to the hand.
Finally, he said, "That is the second time you wouldn't let me
go. I was very annoyed."

She smiled. "I do not apologize. Where would you have
gone—this time?"

He shook his head. "There was some—dream, possibly.
Two forces of Oneness fought over me, and one of them
was—Totality. It could not be fought. A Siren Song of the
mind, sung exactly for *me*. Sola—someone has planned this,
somehow."

She frowned. "The same thought has been coming to me.
But how? And—who? Someone might have learned that I
would have to come here. Someone might have arranged for
you to come. But who could know what the effect of our
meeting would be? I have not spoken your name, aloud, for
years."

He smiled. "Maybe—to a sufficiently astute mind—it was
written all over us. Just in our records. For the same reason
that I knew yours, and you mine."

"Spock—also knew."

"I wonder if anyone counted on *that?*" He pulled her down to sit beside him. "Sola, tell me now. Was there any way in which *you* arranged this?"

She sat very straight. "When I saw the *Enterprise,* I sent a Free Agent code signal requesting it be ordered to turn back."

"Turn back—when you knew who we were, and you needed help?"

"I did not think your starship, nor you, would survive untaken. The *Enterprise* is much too dangerous a weapon to give the Totality. And to give them *you* would be still more dangerous."

"One man?"

"You are known to the galaxy as the Starship Captain who is the symbol and the reality of what takes us to the stars. You are the last man who would choose a Oneness. But if they could claim you—what would it do for their cause?

Kirk shook his head. "Am I the last amoeba? Sola, how do we know that Gailbraith is not right—that we are defending our little, limited lives against the great multicelled experiment in evolution? It was that first little multicelled blob which finally climbed out on land, and up to stars."

"That is the question which sent me back to Zaran," she said.

"To do what?" he asked. "What I never understood is how you could give up *your* starship."

"You risked yours—your command, your career—once to take Spock to Vulcan against a direct Starfleet order. I know Vulcan well enough to guess that it was for his life . . ."

He shrugged. "Then you would know there was no question. It is not the same as giving up the stars for an abstract cause. To free your people?"

"That, and more. I saw that the galaxy would have to deal with Oneness and that Zaran would become the focal point. I believe the Totality has found a way to use the native powers of females of my species to force unity on the missing ships. It may be nearing the solution of how to force it on the galaxy. If it could also unite with other forms of Oneness, such as Gailbraith's—or capture you . . . or both . . . it would take the galaxy."

Kirk started to sit up, found that he couldn't. "I have to warn Spock. In the dream—I remembered that Gailbraith warned me . . . to expect *you*. If he is behind this, if he brought us together—" He caught her hand. *"What* powers of females of your species, Sola?"

"When we bond with a life-mate," she said, "it is a psionic joining. Out of it the female can create a wider psionic unity. Once it was only of the tribe for a hunt. Now certain females might be made to unite a planet, perhaps even a galaxy."

"You?" he asked.

"Unknown," she said in a tone which reminded him of Spock. "But the Totality believes I am at the head of the list. Perhaps even that I will possess a new level of power."

He looked at the meeting of their hands. "Then it would be to their advantage—to bring you a life-mate."

"It has been tried. Various males were 'planted' on me. Without success. Until n—"

He put up a hand and stopped her from saying it. But the hand touched her lips, then her face, then slipped into the tawny hair to pull her down to him. "If that was their plan," he murmured, "make the most of it."

He felt her smile against his mouth.

After a time she lifted her head and looked down to him. "If that is their plan," she managed, "we are playing with anti-matter."

He laughed softly. "We are, anyway." Then a thought struck him and the other part of his dream came back to him. "Sola—is Spock all right?"

Some expression he could not read touched her face. "Spock is—quite all right."

He was remembering now. "In the scoutship he said he was a dead man. And you—knew what he meant. You said only one act would save him. Sola—I can't have understood what you said."

"You understood me perfectly."

"That Spock would have to deal with you in some way? I saw him learn that in the clearing. And you are—not dreamed of in Vulcan philosophy. But then Spock himself was never exactly contemplated in Vulcan philosophy."

"No."

"He would find you—most uncommon." Kirk smiled. "But why not? And with those emotions which of course he does not have, he would be angry with you and with himself over what happened to me. Maybe the primitive Vulcan under that veneer would have liked to break your neck for you—or at least bend it. But Spock didn't do that, obviously." His eyes narrowed, seeing something dark on her jawline. "Or did he? Sola—I thought earlier that when he saw you—it triggered an old Vulcan pattern for him. I hoped I was wrong."

He stopped and she did not answer, letting him work it out. He realized only then that there was some subtle change he had sensed in her, something she had been telling him without words.

"You said—only one act, one choice could save him?"

She nodded. "And I had only one choice, if he was Spock enough to save himself. I made it."

His hand tightened on hers and then released it suddenly, as if he caught himself in some impropriety. "My mistake!" he said.

She pulled her hand away sharply and started to rise. *"Mine,"* she said. *"That* was the risk I took."

His hand shot out and caught her wrist and pulled her down again with surprising power. "Stop that," he ordered. "If you made your choice, you can damn well stay until I understand it."

Now he looked at her very hard and saw the strain, the effort, the pride. "Is it possible," he asked, "that you meant what you said—to *both* of us?"

She laughed then. "They had to send the one man in the galaxy who would know that *that* was the right question."

"Answer me."

"Yes. Always. Exactly."

"Tell me now, exactly."

"Vulcan physiological control can be broken down. By too much mental contact, by Oneness, by personal affinity. Love. Or the need for it, the hope, the longing. And even by the philosophical search for a way out of the Vulcan box," Sola said. "If *you* exist, then Spock's Vulcan theory of non-emotion is already strained to the snapping point. But he has lived with that. If *I* also exist, my "logic" may be the straw which breaks his back."

"Or—his heart?" Kirk said.

"Literally," she said, "he was prepared to die, not to impose the consequences of his state on me—nor on any of your Human crew, who are much too fragile. I was not prepared to let *him* go, either. I told him he would leave you nowhere to go but Oneness. He was not prepared to leave you to that. But he was Vulcan enough to have no choice left—except one. And he was Spock enough to make it."

"You—did it only to save his life?"

"No. I would have done it for that. But that was not my reason. He *is* Spock."

Kirk sighed. "Yes. He is."

She lifted her head. "I had also another reason. There would have been no choice left for us if I had destroyed Spock. There is one now, and it is yours."

"Did you tell *Spock* that?"

"Yes. And that it was not treason."

"Isn't it? Not for *you*, possibly. Sola—did you say that the choice is mine?"

She nodded, suddenly wary. She saw effort in his face.

"Then go to him."

She pulled back as if he had hit her. This time he did sit up, heedless of the pain and of the room's lurching. He pulled her to him and held her as if it was a punishment for both of them. It was. He could not escape the too-specific vision of other arms holding her. And she could not forgive him for telling her to go—nor could she make herself pull away. He did not release her until they were both ravaged, knowing that it was a taste they should not have allowed. Drink deep—or taste not . . .

"Did you suppose I would take you away from him now?" he asked.

She shot to her feet and her eyes were angry. "Yes! He does not require any favors."

"I know what he does not require. And what he *does*. Sola, I have broken my—anatomy—trying to get Spock out of that box. And if *you* have done it—even for a moment—" He shook his head. "If you saw Prometheus chained to his rock, and still keeping on, dragging chains, rock, vultures, and all—and then for a moment he was free . . ."

He held himself up by the strength of her hand and looked at her as if he would break her in half. "Is the choice mine?" he demanded.

She lifted her head and met his eyes. "Yes."

"Then, when you leave this room, you will not come back unless in the line of duty. You do not have to remember that I exist. Whatever might have been, these next days, at least, cannot be mine. You will go to him, and you will be to him—what you are. Will you do it?"

Sola was on her feet suddenly, standing rigidly, as if in the military manner of facing punishment. Her face was the battlefield of some sense that it was flatly impossible—and the sudden realization that it was *not*.

"I did give you my word," she said flatly.

"Not as punishment," he said. "Not if it *is* punishment."

"And if it would *not* be?" she asked, not sparing him, clearly not wanting to.

He set his jaw. "Then go."

"For *him?*" she asked.

He knew that she saw the weakness hitting him again. "Yes," he said. "And for me. You haven't finished with Spock. You may never finish with him. Sola, I am the galaxy's greatest living expert on Spock. If you've seen him begin to shake off the vultures, you could not have eyes for anything else. Not now. I may pin his Vulcan ears back for him"—he was shaking now and he could barely sit up—"later," he said ruefully, and she caught him and eased him back down.

She felt his forehead, smoothed it out with a touch of the life-energy until the shaking quieted. "Idiot," she said. "*I* am the fool. I will go now. But I will be back."

He caught her hand. "No. You gave me the choice."

She met his eyes then. "I cannot answer for what I would feel for the Spock who would exist at the end of those days."

"Don't you suppose I *know* that?" he said harshly. "But don't you know—*I* want to set *that* Spock free, too? I've broken my head to jar that Spock loose, for years."

She merely stood and looked at him, for once at a loss. "You have said the one thing which would make me go—and you have made it impossible."

He grinned weakly. "You'll manage. I want—*that* Sola, too."

"I wanted that Sola—from *you.*"

"I would have liked that," he said. "My fault. I should have tracked you to the ends of the galaxy, years ago."

"Yes," she said, and he heard the edge in her voice. "You should have."

He lifted his head, and he knew that his eyes were angry with her. "*You* knew where *I* was." He jerked his head toward the door. "Call Spock."

"Spock?" she said, startled.

He nodded. "I can afford the luxury."

She stepped to the intercom. "So can *he.*"

Before she could touch it the doors opened and Spock stood in them.

"Mr. Spock, report," Kirk said.

"On the *ship?*" Spock asked involuntarily.

"Certainly on the *ship,* Mr. Spock," Kirk said with a certain wicked innocence. Short of pinning the Vulcan's ears back, that tone would have to do.

"All vital systems appear to be—functional," the Vulcan said, possibly not to be outdone in innocence.

"Including yours, Mr. Spock?" Kirk looked pointedly at the Vulcan himself.

"I was referring primarily to mechanical systems, Captain."

"Indeed. Very well. Carry on, Mr. Spock."

"Sir?" The Vulcan sounded faintly scandalized.

"Dismissed, Mr. Spock. You have—the con, among other things—until further notice. I won't need you."

"Sir," Spock said firmly, beginning to get the picture, and not certain that he liked it. *"I* am entirely—functional."

"I never doubted it," Kirk said. "I, however, am not, at the moment. Get out of here, both of you, and let me loaf."

For a moment he saw Spock catch Sola's eye and see that she was rather proud of both of them.

"I see," Spock said. "Recommendation noted, Captain. I shall, however, be rather busy with command duties. Since you are not fit, I will give you a full report—later."

He started to turn.

"Spock!" Kirk said in a tone which would have cut glass. *"Now,* Mr. Spock."

Spock turned back, but now the private man dropped away and the command officer remained, looking at Kirk with the unspoken respect of their years. "Captain," he said, "we are Condition Seven, under alien mental attack. I must conclude that you are a primary target, perhaps *the* primary target, and that Sola's presence may be related to your danger. Crew members have been made to unlock essential locks and sabotage reporting systems. We have detected on the planet below camouflaged geo-thermal power readings and intelligent life-form readings in a solitary volcano near the clearing where Sola landed. It is doubtless the starship-trap advance base of the Zaran Totality. Our crew is being taken over, and the *Enterprise* will, at the present rate, swiftly fall prey to the Marie Celeste syndrome."

Kirk merely looked at him for a moment, then he swung his legs down and stood up. Sola was close enough to catch him as he fell. . . .

Chapter 14

Spock also was there in a moment to lift the Human back to the diagnostic bed.

"It's all right, Spock," Kirk murmured. "Just—legs wouldn't hold me."

"Be still," Spock ordered. He signaled for McCoy.

Sola was putting her hands on Kirk's face. McCoy came through the door as if he had already been under full warp drive. He did not even pause but ran a scanner over Kirk. Kirk waved them both away.

"First," Kirk said, "check Gailbraith. It's just coming to me, what I half-remembered in the dream. Gailbraith was out of isolation before. He warned me before we left the ship that I would find what I needed—on the planet. He came to me in the Pool One area."

"Why did you not tell me this before?" Spock asked.

Kirk shook his head. "There was some form of mental contact. I believe that he blocked the memory. It began to come back while I was unconscious."

"Why did the Ambassador come to you in Pool One?"

Kirk sighed rather reluctantly. "I was drowning, Mr. Spock."

"I am a fool," Spock said. He stepped to the intercom. "Security to Sickbay."

"I'm all right, Mr. Spock. No damage done."

Spock looked at him bleakly. "How would you *know* that? You were exposed in a vulnerable condition to an alien mind force of unknown powers—which was powerful enough to make you forget the incident. Moreover, the isolation-locks on the VIP Quarters cannot be released from the inside. Gailbraith must already have controlled some member of the *Enterprise* crew who unlocked them for him."

Kirk grimaced. "You're right. Run a full personnel check."

"There is something else," Spock said. "There have been times when you have been in mortal danger and *I* have sensed it. This time *I* sensed nothing. But your distress *was* answered."

Kirk frowned. "You are saying—I was in touch with Gailbraith's Oneness more than with you. You believe I am being drawn into it?"

"If we are to fight it, we must, in logic, acknowledge the possibility."

"It is possible to develop a certain taste for Oneness, Mr. Spock, as you know. However, I believe I am still—the last amoeba."

"Captain," Sola said, "I have become a danger to you and possibly to Spock."

There still managed to be some trace of a wry amusement in Kirk's eyes. "We'll manage."

She shook her head. "You do not understand. I am a Zaran female. If I am irrevocably drawn toward a life-bond commitment my powers become an unknown, not under my control. They may amplify any Oneness effect—draw you into it against your will. The Totality may be able to use me. I am a danger to the whole ship."

The amusement left. Kirk looked at her gravely. "What can we do about that?"

She stood straighter. "I must leave the ship."

"No," Kirk said flatly. "Whatever we do, it will not be *that*."

"Spock," she said. "Logic. There is no alternative."

"No," Spock said. "Someone has been at some pains to arrange our encounter. If we attempt to evade the engagement, we will doubtless have to face the issue again in a form which may be still more dangerous."

"In a word, Spock," McCoy interpreted, "logic be hanged. You won't let her go."

"One cannot hang logic, Doctor," Spock answered. "But one can be sorely tempted."

"You won't let her go?" McCoy persisted.

"No."

"Spock is right," Kirk said. "It *is* logic, even if it is also what we want. We have to make our stand—together."

"You, too?" McCoy asked.

"Do you say 'go,' Bones?"

McCoy looked at Sola wryly, as if knowing how much simpler his life—and his job—could have been. "No, confound it," he said.

Kirk smiled. "Mr. Spock, you will follow my original request. Sola, I will ask you to assist Mr. Spock in this crisis. Dismissed."

Spock looked at Kirk and understood entirely.

"I do not require any—assistance," Spock said.

Kirk's gesture stressed that he was flat on his back. "You're not getting any. I'll take it up with you—later, Mr. Spock. Get going. That is an order."

McCoy looked from one to the other and read them like a scanner. "One second," he interposed. "While you have been dealing with—whatever—we've got more trouble. Mr. Dobius appears to have been taken over by a Oneness. Or, maybe—I may be going crazy—but I'd almost say he was taken over by *two*."

"How, Bones?" Kirk shifted instantly back to the command mode.

"When I checked him—and went looking for Spock—one brain half was attuned to Gailbraith's Oneness. The other showed some strange, similar pattern but *not* the *same* pattern. Maybe Sola's Totality?"

"You may be right, Bones," Kirk said. "Get everything you can on that second pattern."

"I just tried. No luck. In those few minutes both strange brain patterns faded. Mr. Dobius now seems to be perfectly normal."

"You believe the effect was temporary?" Sola asked.

"I wish I *did*," McCoy said gloomily. "I think it's still there—but with no visible symptoms now. It has—masked itself. I think even Mr. Dobius doesn't know it—but I believe he still is or can be under someone's control. And there is no way at all to detect it now."

"Are you saying," Kirk asked, "that if someone—say, *me*—was affected, he might not know it—and after some brief period it would not be detectable?"

"I believe," McCoy said glumly, "that is what I *said.*"

Kirk again tried to move and knew the utter frustration of helplessness. His ship was under attack. Spock was facing perhaps the crisis of his life. They were quite possibly holding a finger in the dike which could crumble to engulf the galaxy in Oneness. He himself might already have started to crumble on that front.

"Bones," he said, "you'd better give me whatever it takes to get me on my feet. I can't sit this one out."

"I'm a doctor, not a magician," McCoy said. "You're staying put."

"Bones—" Kirk said warningly.

McCoy was making adjustments on a spray hypo. "This may make you feel a little better. It's not going to erase cumulative stress and near-fatal shock. And I don't know a cure for what else ails you." He flashed a glance at Sola.

"That's all right, Bones." Kirk started to sit up, but the room started to rotate.

"Mr. Spock," he said, "you have your orders. Go check the crew by any means which you, Sola, or the medical department can devise. Set double watches, no one to perform a critical function alone. You and Sola check each other. Don't come back, except in line of duty."

Spock merely looked at him for a long moment, and Kirk thought for that moment that he would refuse. "Captain," he said finally, and turned to go, gathering Sola up with him without touching her.

She looked back for a moment at Kirk, as if to acknowledge that she was obeying his choice. But he saw that the current was still there between her and Spock, regardless of any effort by either one of them to resist it. He knew then that he had been right. Before anything else, she had to finish with Spock, if she could . . . and he had to make certain that the *pon farr* was not merely eased but finished, and that Spock would live.

And—there was some subliminal thought which told Kirk that whoever had planned this for Kirk and Sola could not have reckoned with Spock. Did it give the three of them some subtle advantage if she was also drawn to both? Or did it double their danger?

The door closed behind Sola and Spock.

"What was *that* all about?" McCoy grumbled.

"What would *you* diagnose, Bones?"

McCoy snorted. "What *I* diagnose isn't even conceivable." He ran the scanner over Kirk. "If he weren't a Vulcan . . ." McCoy shrugged.

"*If* he weren't?"

"Love. Hate. Both. But he *is,* and you had better just *tell* me."

"That's close enough, Bones."

"But she's in love with *you!*" McCoy caught himself. "Sorry. But it was written all over her. And it looked to me like—you, too."

Kirk sighed. "Bones, what if she is Spock's first real love? I wish I didn't think that she's—my *last.*"

McCoy groaned. "I *said* it wasn't even conceivable. That bad?"

"That bad."

Kirk felt the stimulant working and moved more cautiously now to get to his feet. The weakness and pain settled on him like a weight of impossibility. He knew then that he should not get up, but he bit down on the agony and did not let McCoy see the extent of his weakness. He could move because he had to move. But he knew it could not last. He started to dress.

"*I* should have my head examined for even letting you think of getting up," McCoy said.

"Have you examined *mine?*" Kirk asked.

McCoy winced. "That was my second morsel of agony for you," he said. "After I checked Dobius, I ran the scanner tapes of your unconscious period. There were times in which both mental patterns—the Oneness and the Totality—started to displace your own."

Kirk looked at him carefully. "Did one succeed?"

McCoy shrugged. "No way to tell. It looked to me like maybe one held off the other. Maybe it was a stalemate. But I can't be sure. The readings are normal now—but so is Dobius. Jim—it's a second reason you shouldn't go running around the ship."

"It's the first reason I have to, Bones," Kirk said. "What's my alternative? Lie there and be taken in my sleep—if I haven't been already?"

McCoy looked at him gravely. "Jim, what if you *have* been?"

Kirk moved down the corridor. Every step was an effort beyond his endurance.

There was no answer to McCoy's question. Was it possible that Kirk already belonged to a Oneness—Gailbraith's, or the other, the Totality? He could detect no sign, but there was nothing to say that he *would* know. Suppose they were holding him on a long line, just waiting to pull the strings? Certainly he had had the feeling in his dream that two forces warred for him—and now all of McCoy's instruments agreed.

Unless he could resolve that, Kirk could not command the ship. Nor could he be certain that anyone else could. If some power of Sola's people were the catalyst which the Totality could use—then was Spock in the most danger of all? The Vulcan also sailed perilously close to whatever unity bonding with her would require.

Kirk turned into the Pool One area. Perhaps to come here was foolishness. He could have gone to the VIP Guest Quarters, bearded Gailbraith in his den. He wanted to try this.

He stood by the pool, then finally had to sit down, projecting in some way he couldn't name "Here I am. Come!"

It took less than one minute. Gailbraith entered through the door.

Kirk started to stand up, had to think better of it. "Ambassador. So you do have the run of the ship?"

"Did you expect otherwise?" The hard gray eyes inspected Kirk with a kind of reproach. "You came here for some more definite purpose than to establish that. I see you are aware you should not have stirred from bed."

Kirk shrugged. "I have no choice. You have taken some of my people. How many? Whom?"

"Would you expect me to answer?"

"I expect you to release them."

"Captain," Gailbraith said, "does it not occur to you that there must be a reason why all ships have been taken in this sector—and why yours, carrying us, is still free?"

"Are you saying that *you* are fighting the Totality for us?"

Gailbraith smiled. "No, Captain. Not for *you.*"

"But you *are* fighting it?"

"Where the longing for Oneness exists, Captain, it is a vacuum which will be filled, one way or the other. That is where the takeover—of a ship or a galaxy—begins. At present I have filled some of your own voids with myself. Not all of them. And I have not saved all of your people."

"The Totality has some of my crew?"

Gailbraith nodded.

"How can I stop it?"

"You cannot."

"*You* can?"

"Conceivably. Not in any way you would care for."

"Are you saying my choice is between possession by the Totality, or possession by *you?*"

"That is crudely put, but essentially correct."

"And if I won't be possessed?"

"But you *will* be. Captain, a trial is in progress here. This ship, the planet below, do not necessarily look like the battlefield on which the fate of the galaxy will be decided. Nonetheless, that is what they *are.*"

"You are *against* the Totality?" Kirk asked.

"Captain, I am *for* evolution. However, it remains to be seen what the essential direction of evolution *is.* As the man who condemned you to this trial has said, there are also blind alleys in evolution. One of us, Captain, is an amoeba—or a dinosaur. Here we will find out which."

"And then?"

"If you are the amoeba, you will come to me and become the future. And I will have decided that the turning point is here, and Oneness is to be loosed on the galaxy in my lifetime."

"Do you mean—through the Totality?" Kirk asked.

"The Totality has the means. I do not."

"Force? If I know nothing else, I know that *that* is yesterday."

"Is it force to offer tomorrow irresistibly?"

"Tomorrow has been the excuse for every atrocity."

"And the fuel of every advance to the stars. Now, perhaps, the direction of advance is—beyond love."

"Is there no love in your Oneness?" Kirk asked.

"There is the extension of self. All parts become valued, necessary. But that force of passion for the individual loved one who can see into our solitude and illuminate our sameness with his difference—that passion is not ours."

"Why, then, should you want to bring any particular man or woman in?" Kirk asked.

"There is—remembrance of individual choice, Captain. We are yet young in the universe. And there is power. Certain minds would add to our strength, perhaps decisively." Then he looked at Kirk, almost with amusement. "Apart from that, there is the Job factor."

"What?"

"You are the most faithful servant of the old order, Captain, and as in the original story, he whom you serve has delivered you into the hands of temptation. It always seemed to me a rather poor reward for virtue."

Kirk nodded. "As I recall, Job lost his wife, family, flocks, herds, herdsmen, and his health, strength, friends, comforters. I don't think I care to apply for the part."

Gailbraith shook his head. "You have been cast, Captain, long ago, as I have. The final trial must always be against the best."

"And what is your role?"

"I am the Devil," Gailbraith said. "Or else I am becoming a god."

Kirk looked at Gailbraith very carefully. There was no madness in him. He was a new order of life, possibly even *the* new order of life, and whether he was the future or not, he was wholly committed to summoning the future. But he would decide here which future to summon.

"Whichever you are—god or devil," Kirk said, "I have a proposition. I will consider your solution. I will experience it to such extent as I can without being captured. If I become convinced, I will be yours. But until I do, you will help me to protect me and mine from the Totality—advise, instruct, protect, block. You will not make your decision *about* the Totality until you have seen also, fully, the power of love, which exists on this ship. And you will, with your powers of god or devil—which I experienced today—help me with minor things. Such as being able to stand up."

Gailbraith laughed. "What would have happened if Job had had the gall to ask the Devil to heal him of his boils—without even demanding his soul?"

"If the Devil were smart," Kirk said, "he would have done it."

Gailbraith nodded. "Yes. He would have. I accept your terms, Captain, until further notice—with the exception that I cannot guarantee that you will not be captured by our Oneness—or the Totality. You are vulnerable, especially now, and it is a tricky business. However, I will make no deliberate attempt to take you or keep you against your will—without giving warning first. Agreed?"

Kirk nodded. "Agreed."

Gailbraith came toward him. "Experience Oneness, then, at least the first level, and be whole." He put his powerful hands on contact points on Kirk's face and head, on reflex points on the injured arm.

The boundaries of the me/not-me began to dissolve. Kirk sensed the magnitude of the man who had been able to absorb other "me's" and remain the head, the brain, the passion. Then even the boundaries of the body seemed to dissolve and he could feel the tremendous pouring of the wholeness of the One into his ravaged body. Tissues and cells were rebuilt; life-energy fields rebalanced; strength, hope, desire revitalized. He was One. He was god. They were together. They were born again, one and indivisible—

Chapter 15

Spock's head jerked up from the science station and turned to look at Sola. She was all right.

Spock stood up, raggedly, and she followed him as he plunged into the turbolift.

"What is it?" she asked.

"Jim!" The word was a croak in his throat. "Pool One," he said to the turbolift.

They arrived to find Gailbraith bending over Kirk. They both appeared to be locked into some abnormal state, some peculiar intensity. Spock did not stand on ceremony. He pulled Gailbraith's hands off the contact points and flung him halfway across the room. Kirk groaned. Spock put out his own hands to replace the touch. "We are one," he murmured in the old formula of the Vulcan mind-touch.

But they were not one. He recoiled in shock from a presence he could barely recognize—a presence which was still Kirk, but which was almost over the edge into irrevocable Oneness. Slowly, with infinite patience and terror Spock reached out to draw his friend back from that edge. *"T'hyla,"* he said, "Jim! Your path is here."

He felt the wordless resistance, some part of which merely wanted to go and leave Spock what he most needed. There was an image of the woman whom Kirk had required to go back to Spock. There was still some large, stubborn remainder which was pure Starship Captain and which took this way to fight for all their lives and for his ship.

It was to that part, finally, that Spock spoke. "The ship has been effectively sabotaged in vital systems. We cannot leave orbit. You are needed on the Bridge."

He felt the mind snap back into the familiar pattern. "Spock?"

"Captain."

After a moment Spock released the meld. In that moment he saw in the Captain's mind the nature of the bargain Kirk had struck.

He pulled back and looked hard into the Human's hazel eyes. "It is as close to selling your soul as you have ever come," Spock said.

Kirk took a very deep breath. "It is as close to losing it. Thank you, Mr. Spock." He reached to feel the injured arm. "At least the Devil keeps his word," he said.

He stood up then, and Spock looked at him in astonishment, seeing the old energy, the old sparkle.

Spock reached and stripped back the sleeve over the injured arm. The spray dressing was peeling off of new, healthy skin. There were no scars.

Spock turned to look at Gailbraith, who appeared to have recovered from the shock of separation. Gailbraith bowed faintly. "Mr. Spock, I believe I can advise even you on some of the finer points of resisting the Oneness of the Totality."

"I require no instruction," Spock said coldly.

"I *do,*" Kirk said. "Let's see about those sabotaged systems, Mr. Spock."

He led off with the old energy, and Gailbraith joined them.

Chapter 16

McCoy headed for the Bridge. He should have informed Spock before that Kirk was on the loose, and he had better do it now and face the Vulcan music in person.

McCoy should never have let Kirk up at all, and he was kicking himself for it. But he had seen catastrophe gaining on them from all directions, and there was no denying that Kirk was the master of the impossible solution.

McCoy would have told Spock sooner, but the Catullan biochemist, Vrrr, had staggered into Sickbay with unexplained symptoms, and McCoy had put her on the brain-scan. This time he caught the pattern he had learned to recognize as the Zaran Totality before it had disappeared. Apparently, the attempt by the Totality to take over Vrrr had produced some near-fatal conflict with the notoriously independent Catullan mind. For a while McCoy thought he would lose her, and he labored to stabilize her from symptoms of deep shock. Eventually, the Totality pattern faded, she breathed evenly, then suddenly looked at McCoy with apparent sanity out of her great cat-eyes. But he was not certain whether Vrrr had won—or lost finally.

His gut-hunch was that she had lost. He put her under guard—not that he could tell whether the guard was reliable. There was no way to detect possession by either the Totality or Gailbraith's Oneness. And there was no way for McCoy to fight it. He felt certain that large numbers of crew people were being taken. And it had occurred to him, belatedly, that Kirk would go to confront the problem in the person of Gailbraith.

McCoy went to tell Spock. But it was all four of them he found as the turbolift decanted him on the Bridge simultaneously with the other one bearing Spock, Sola, Kirk, and Gailbraith. McCoy found that the Ambassador made his own hackles inexplicably rise, the short hairs standing up quite literally at the back of his neck, as if he faced not a civilized man but some ancient jungle enemy.

Maybe he *did,* McCoy thought. Maybe long ago—perhaps there was an earlier battle between Oneness and individuality, and somewhere some last battle had decided it, at least for a time. And at that moment perhaps the loneliness, the splendor, the love, were born—and the occasional longing for some lost Eden of Oneness.

Now the tribal Oneness rose again in a new form, and McCoy stood at bay against it, as doctor and as man. His medicine was unable to reclaim its victims. He saw the look on Spock's face and knew that Gailbraith's Oneness must have touched Kirk. . . . Then McCoy took one look at Kirk, who looked as if he had been freshly overhauled—unless you noticed the strain around the eyes. McCoy ran the scanner over him. Then he ran it again, not believing the readings.

"What in God's name have you *done?"* he demanded. The scanner showed perfect health—except for traces of some new shock which would have stopped most men cold.

Kirk had a slightly stunned look behind the eyes, but he managed to focus on McCoy. "It's all right, Bones. I struck—a kind of bargain with the Devil."

"I believe it," McCoy said sourly. He peeled Kirk's sleeve

up and saw the newly healed flesh. Perfect. Impossible. And McCoy didn't like it.

"It's a healing concentration of the force of Gailbraith's Oneness, Bones," Kirk said. "Don't worry, I haven't been absorbed. Yet. Although it may be that Mr. Spock pulled me out just in time." His eyes looked haunted, but he snapped himself into the command mode and faced all of them.

"We have no knowledge or technology with which to fight the attempt by the Totality to take over this ship. The Zaran Totality is the most dangerous form of Oneness which the galaxy faces. Sola believes the Totality is using the psionic powers of mate-bonded females of her species to weld larger and larger groups together. She does not know how to stop it. It has taken every ship it has attacked in this sector. If it gets the *Enterprise,* it can wipe out the physical resistance of Sola's resistance movement on Zaran. And it can destroy other planets if they offer resistance. If the Totality gets Sola as a bonded female, it may not even need to use much physical force. None of us knows anything about Oneness. Gailbraith does. There is a saying about the only way to fight fire. I have adopted the principle. I will use Gailbraith's Oneness against the Totality. Gailbraith offered certain assistance."

"At what price?" Spock asked suddenly, and McCoy saw that the Vulcan's hackles were up, too, probably worse than his own. God knew what the Vulcan had pulled Kirk out of. A mind-link with Gailbraith?

Kirk faced Spock squarely. "I have agreed to experience the Oneness, and to—consider the alternative."

"There *is no* alternative," Spock said. "You are what you are, and your essence cannot endure any surrender to Oneness. There is an adage also about playing with fire—and getting burned. We must solve this apart from Gailbraith, or we will have surrendered the prime target in advance. *You.*" Spock turned to Gailbraith. "His sacrifice is not acceptable to any of us. You will consider it the gallant offer of a man medically unfit to make it, and you will withdraw."

"No, Mr. Spock," Gailbraith said quietly. "I will not."

Spock turned to Kirk. "Withdraw the offer."

Kirk looked at the Vulcan gravely. "I'm sorry, Mr. Spock. I can't do that."

"Doctor McCoy," Spock said, "the Captain is medically unfit for command following severe injury and an intense form of alien mind contact which may have rendered him the captive of an inimical alien power. I must insist that you certify him medically unfit to command."

"Spock," McCoy said, "I couldn't agree more." He saw the Vulcan's look of gratitude and quickly shook his head. "I can't do it, Spock. No evidence. He checks out in perfect health. And I can't detect the effects of Oneness—in *anybody. You* could be captive, too, for all I know. I don't like his bargain, either. But I have no medical authority to stop him."

"Thank you, Bones," Kirk said. He reached for a moment and put a hand on McCoy's shoulder. "Don't worry. Let's get on with it."

Then Kirk dropped down the stairs to the command chair. It was Sola who followed him.

"You are not to consider it," she said very quietly.

"What?" Kirk asked.

"Going off into the night—or the Oneness. It will not solve our problem."

He looked up at her. "At the moment I am primarily concerned with saving my ship. If you want to help me, continue as agreed."

"The agreement did not include your bargain with the Devil."

"Necessity makes strange bedfellows—as you know," he said. "There are some prices which have to be paid, and this is one of them."

He turned to Gailbraith. "Ambassador, can you detect the rate at which the Totality is gaining control of the *Enterprise* crew?"

"Yes," Gailbraith said.

"How long do we have?" Kirk asked.

McCoy saw Spock turn from the science station. It was the question Kirk would normally have asked *him*.

Gailbraith shrugged. "They control key stations now. At the present rate they can have an effective majority in three hours, and the most resistant minds in six."

"How can we fight it?" Kirk asked Gailbraith.

"You will not like either of the answers," Gailbraith said.

"I don't like the *questions*," Kirk said. "Say it."

"My Oneness can contest for each soul. It has, in fact, been doing so. I control a number of your crew which I will not specify. At your order others would join without resistance.

You could choose the Devil, you know—my Oneness rather than the Totality—and order your crew to do likewise."

"You're right, I don't like it," Kirk said. "What is the other answer?"

Gailbraith turned to look at Sola. "The Zaran female is amplifying the effect of the Totality, and to some extent even of my Oneness. The more she remains in your presence, Captain, the more she is drawn toward bonding and the more dangerous she becomes to all of you. You must choose between her and your ship."

"I like that still less," Kirk said. "Find a third choice."

Gailbraith shrugged. "Accept the trial which the Totality sets as a challenge."

"What trial?" McCoy interjected.

Gailbraith turned to indicate Sola. "In this rather interesting package, we have all of Zaran. She is the heart of Zaran resistance, and it would be her power which would give the Totality a psionic weapon to start a chain reaction of Oneness. As she goes, so goes her planet—and quite possibly the galaxy. Has it not occurred to any of you that we are all very conveniently met here?"

"It has occurred to me that *you* arranged it," Kirk said. "You knew she would be here. And you brought *me*."

"That is true, as far as it goes," Gailbraith said. "Did it occur to you to wonder *why?*"

"To bring out my latent bonding-powers," Sola said. "It has been tried before, but not effectually. Ambassador, was it you who chose to send Captain Kirk and the *Enterprise?*"

"Yes," Gailbraith said. "With some knowledge of the Totality's purpose."

"The Ambassador is astute," Sola said. "And he is right. We have been overreached, and I must leave the ship. I will take the scoutship." She turned to go.

"No," Kirk said flatly, and Spock did not move aside from blocking her path to the turbolift.

"It may be rather late even for that," Gailbraith added. "I would expect that at any moment we may hear from the Totality with the terms of the challenge."

"What else do they want from her?" McCoy grumbled. Gailbraith turned the steel-gray eyes on him and McCoy felt the sheer power of the man.

"She is their key to bringing Oneness to the galaxy in my lifetime, Doctor," Gailbraith said.

"And *you* want to bring Oneness in your lifetime," Kirk said to Gailbraith.

"Yes, Captain."

"But at what cost?" Kirk protested. "If your goal is right, can it not win without force?"

Gailbraith shrugged. "That has been my belief. But to win without force may take a thousand years—or a million. Captain, if I could offer you, say, peace in your lifetime and forever, but at a cost—would you not be tempted?"

"I might be, Ambassador," Kirk said, "but I have learned that some costs cannot be paid. The use of force destroys any benefit which can come from it."

"I wish I were quite so certain, or so innocent."

Kirk looked at him thoughtfully. "Is that the question you came here to answer, Gailbraith? You also are not here by accident. Is it that the Totality needs something from you? Or do you need something from the Totality?"

"How perceptive, Captain. Both."

"And you *both* need something from *me*—from *us!*" Kirk divined.

Gailbraith nodded. "It is a triangle, Captain, a fateful triangle met here to decide the fate of the galaxy for a million years. We who have chosen Oneness cannot alone bring it to the galaxy in my lifetime. For that we would require the methods of the Totality. The Totality also requires our help—or our neutrality at least. Collectively those of us who have formed diverse kinds of Oneness by choice might stand against the Totality. We would be a plurality of Onenesses, against the single engulfing Totality. The conflict might last for millennia. And while it lasted you singletons would also find room to exist as amoebas. But if I become convinced that the Totality's solution can work, and I decide to bring my kind to join it—we may spare the galaxy a million years of conflict and agony."

Kirk shook his head. "You would extinguish greatness— and love. There is no room for diversity in Oneness, no spark which jumps across a gulf of difference to create . . . ecstasy."

"*That,* Captain," Gailbraith said, "may be the third point

of the triangle—and the essence of the trial: love versus Oneness. Sola's people have the capacity for Oneness—if any species does. You, your friends, your ship, are the distilled essence of the opposition. The test case is, perhaps, of the power of love."

"It has won before," Kirk said.

"And lost," Gailbraith answered, "many times. I believe you will lose, Captain, for you are torn in two directions. The impossibility of your situation will, finally, bring you to *me.*"

"Gailbraith," Kirk said, "you have promised to help me save my ship—at least until the final decision. I will hold you to that. And I charge you to make your decision carefully. For if you join the Totality, there is no turning back and no alternative. But if you resist and offer individuals the chance to choose your Oneness, or some other, or none, then you preserve your freedom—and ours. Now—how can I contact the Totality?"

"I expect that the Totality will contact *you,*" Gailbraith said in a tone of warning.

Chapter 17

As if on cue the turbolift doors opened on the heels of Gailbraith's words, and Kirk looked up to find an alien presence on his Bridge.

The lone man who stood there might have commanded a galaxy—and it was quite possible now that he *would*.

He had been designed for command by some genius genetic sculptor of long ago who had managed to be both selective and lucky. The tall, massive, broad-shouldered body was a portrait in power. The coppery, gold-flecked eyes were hypnotic. The man's face and body were the essence of maleness, of maleness raised to the point of superdominance, as if that sculptor had carved a face and a stance to represent the essence of the conqueror—or of the unconquerable.

The man looked as if he had been cast in bronze, with gold highlights in the eyes and a copper-bronze mass of untamed hair.

There was some disturbing familiarity about the man's face, as if Kirk should have recognized it for more reasons than he did. The face itself was seldom photographed. But Kirk knew it to be the face of a man who had once been presumed dead for more than two hundred years. The man was legend. And he was the enemy.

"Soljenov of the Totality, I presume," Kirk said.

The big man bowed fractionally. He looked not much older than Kirk, but even counting only time outside the long-sleep of the long-jump ship, he was decades older. The youthfulness must be the gift of an undying vitality, and of the combined life-force of the Totality. Kirk had felt the power of such force through Gailbraith, and he did not want to have to fight it in this man.

"Captain Kirk," Soljenov said in a voice which was deep and resonant with authority—a single voice which spoke for many.

"You have come aboard my ship without notice or permission," Kirk said. "State your purpose."

Soljenov nodded. "You note that I have been able to do so without alerting any of your alarm systems. Those who should have responded to warning lights have not. Those who could have responded were prevented from seeing them. For many purposes, Captain, I control your ship *now*."

"No one controls my ship but me," Kirk said. "At need she will be destroyed."

"Even that may already be beyond your power, Captain. But if it were not, would you prefer to destroy your crew, rather than have them live happily in the new world of Totality? Are you so prejudiced—when your primary mission is to seek out the new? Or do you perhaps fondly hope that you could transport your crew to the planet below—and that they, or you, could survive there? I assure you, it is not an alternative."

"There is always an alternative to surrender," Kirk said. "And history has shown that surrender or appeasement of any totality is not an alternative to destruction—merely a preliminary."

"My predecessors were crude, Captain. I am not. I knew

centuries ago that what they proclaimed as oneness was not factually a Oneness at all, but the worst of all possible systems for brutalizing the many for the benefit of the few. I swore to find the reality of Oneness, and with their psychic research which I was able to expand, I found the beginnings. It took the destruction of my immediate world to drive me out to the stars, where I would find the second interlocking piece of the puzzle. Zaran."

"Is there a third piece?" Kirk asked.

Soljenov laughed. "How perceptive of you, Captain. The third piece is itself an interlocking of the forces met here today. The Ambassador is quite right. I have called you to a challenge."

"And if I do not accept?"

"I'm afraid I said nothing about offering you a choice."

Kirk pressed the intercom button. "Security to Bridge." He had not much faith now in the useful arrival of Security, but he saw Spock move in behind the Master of the Totality.

"What is the nature of the challenge?" Kirk asked, stalling.

"But you are not to know that, in detail, either." Soljenov smiled. "I am afraid I am not nearly so civilized as your personal Devil." He bowed faintly to Gailbraith. "However, you may assume that it is a trial of the central issue—of the question of Oneness, as such. Sola's species, and her line of female inheritance, have a remarkable capacity for Oneness. She has undiscovered powers which I know can unite a world, finally even a galaxy . . ."

"One moment," Sola cut in, stepping to confront Soljenov. "I will not be a party to this. There is no one here for whom I will accept the mating challenge. Nor will I, under any circumstance, serve the Totality. Go now with those who will serve you willingly, and let my people go."

"My dear," Soljenov said, "I have so arranged things that you also will have no choice."

"I will never bond," she said. "I will not undertake mate-hunt. I will not deliver my people, nor the galaxy, into your power."

Soljenov merely smiled. "The art of arranging the inevitable merely requires a knowledge of the unendurable. You *will* hunt your mate in the ancient way. And when your powers are roused, you *will* serve."

Soljenov bowed fractionally, touched a medallion he wore

on a chain, and disappeared from the Bridge in a variation of a transporter shimmer.

"What did you mean, 'mate-hunt'?" Kirk asked quickly.

Sola turned to face him. "It is the custom which provokes the hormonal and psionic responses which lead to life-bonding. The male who believes that a female has begun to desire him for bonding takes himself—or is taken by someone who has a stake in the bonding—such as those who wish to bond a recalcitrant pride-queen—into the most dangerous area of the jungle. If the female is sufficiently called, she hunts him there. It is a life-or-death choice. The hunt raises the intensity of the psionic attraction to the point needed for bonding. The two become one, not in Gailbraith's way or the Totality's, but in love. The longer the male remains free, the stronger the ultimate bond. But the female seeks to find him quickly, for it is the only solitary hunt which is permitted—and required. It is dangerous for both, and he is prey also to other predators."

"And there is no one here for whom you would accept mate-hunt?" Kirk asked.

She said nothing—perhaps because it was plain enough that Soljenov heard anything they said, through some means—perhaps some member of the Bridge crew who was already part of the Totality. Kirt tried to read her eyes.

Her tawny eyes were the last thing he saw on the Bridge. He sensed the aura of an alien transporter effect beginning—and in a moment it had taken him.

Suddenly Kirk was picking himself up off the floor of a jungle clearing and he heard the sounds of the ominous biological overload which was the planet below. Then he knew that Soljenov's trap had closed.

He was alone, unarmed, still in the light slacks, slippers, and Sickbay robe in which he had gone to meet Gailbraith. He did not have a communicator, and in that thick biological soup a single Human life-form reading would be impossible for the ship to trace.

He was quite alone and lost on one of the most dangerous planets in the galaxy. Sola and Spock would have to look for him there—although that was now the last thing she should do. He did not believe that she would turn her back on him—although he would have ordered it if he could.

But even if Sola broke her vow and came to hunt him, there was no way that she, or Spock, could find where to begin.

He heard the coughing of a large cat-type predator, close, and he moved off quietly in the other direction.

Doubtless in the direction of more werewolves . . .

Chapter 18

McCoy swore.

He seemed to be the only one who had breath for it. Spock, after an instant of staring at the empty command seat, seized on the controls of the science station with the excessively quiet deliberation which McCoy had learned to read too well. "Full sensor scan," Spock ordered.

Sola turned without a word to the turbolift doors. Spock stood up and caught her wrist, stopping her. "Where would you look?" he asked.

"I am a Huntress of Zaran."

"A trail must have a beginning," Spock said. "It may be hours, if ever, before I can pinpoint a single Human life-form reading."

Sola looked directly into his eyes. "If the bonding has

begun, there will be a tenuous thread of directional awareness."

"You said there was no one here for whom you would accept mate-hunt," Spock said.

She lifted her head, "I lied, Mr. Spock. Twice."

"Very well," Spock said. "I will go with you."

She shook her head. "Not possible. It would disturb the mechanism by which I must find him, alone."

"He is my Captain, and my responsibility."

"No, Spock. This time he is mine. Let me go before he dies there."

Spock released her wrist. "Take this," he said, giving her his communicator and his phaser. "Will you use the transporter?"

"No. I'll cruise in the scout to pick up a trace. There is an area in the equatorial zone near where I landed before which is the center of gigantism—the most dangerous area."

"I know it," Spock said.

She turned to the turbolift.

But it was at that moment that Spock disappeared in the same alien transporter shimmer.

At that point even McCoy couldn't raise an oath. And he suddenly realized that the Vulcan had left himself unarmed and without communicator.

"Now *which one* are you going to go after?" McCoy asked Sola. If the Totality heard him or Uhura looked at him with a wild surmise, he did not care. It would be plain enough in a moment why both men had been taken.

"Apparently, Doctor, that is what the Totality wishes to learn," Gailbraith said.

"They will not learn that from my action, gentlemen," Sola said. "There is only one option."

But she did not name it, and she turned through the turbolift doors without another word. McCoy considered trying to stop her, decided against it. Not only was it likely to be futile, but the Totality could always take her anyway.

Sulu was already on the Helm intercom. "Chief Engineer Scott to Bridge, urgent," he said. "Mr. Scott, the Captain and Mr. Spock have vanished. You are in command."

And under his breath McCoy heard the Oriental Helmsman mutter, "I hope!"

McCoy was left looking at Gailbraith. *"You* could find

him," McCoy said. "The Captain, at least. You had some link with him."

Gailbraith shrugged. "No one asked me."

"I'm asking," McCoy said.

"What are you offering?"

McCoy stood up straight and locked eyes with the Ambassador. "What have I got that you want?"

Gailbraith smiled. "Perhaps the usual terms, Doctor. Your soul . . . ?"

McCoy jerked his head toward the turbolift doors. "Come with me."

Chapter 19

Sola set the scoutship down in the clearing where they had made their stand against the wolflings. She had no clear certainty that she could pick up a trail from there, but the tenuous sense of directional awareness which she felt at some subliminal level suggested that her quarry had been set down somewhere in that vicinity. One quarry, at least. She was not certain now which one.

The clearing was deserted. She stripped down to jungle hunt gear. In the hunt the skin became sensor and warning system, sometimes the channel of the directional sense. It must be bared to the last reasonable inch. Nor could she afford to use the sophisticated Federation protective devices which the scoutship carried. On second thought, she put one in a light pouch slung on her low belt. She took her recharged wrist coil, Spock's communicator and phaser, and a large and very forthright knife. There were times when nothing else would do.

She opened the doors of the scout, ran a few feet, leaped up to a low-hanging branch, and swung up into the lower terrace of tree-paths.

There was a sudden rush from the clearing's edge, and the pack of animals which must have been lying up, hoping for the return of their prey, snapped at the space she had just left.

She was pleased to see them. At least they had not picked up the track of her own quarry.

She quested for the direction now, moving through the lower terrace in a widening search-spiral. The interlocking life-tree branches were wide and easy at that level. She ran, jumped, swung by old reflex, without necessity of thought. This was virtually a sister-planet of Zaran, its evolution strikingly parallel, its hazards largely known to her—although she was aware that to push that assumption too far courted disaster. There would be differences, and they could be deadly.

Meanwhile, she could cover ground through the trees at least two or three times as fast as a man on the ground who had to cope with underbrush and all predators. Here only the great cats and one or two other rather unpleasant adversaries could come.

She hoped that Kirk would have had sense enough to follow her example and take to the trees. An active man could move here, if not with her skill, at least with somewhat better odds of survival than on the ground.

She performed the mental disciplines of the hunt, the focusing of all senses, physical and psionic. And at the end she permitted herself to acknowledge that this *was* mate-hunt. The commitment, once made, was irrevocable. It could end only with mating—or her death. But there was no choice. The directional signal would not work for anything less—might not work even so, given the briefness of contact and the division of heart she had permitted.

Still, there was no hesitation in her heart. She reached for the mate-signal; then she stopped and stood quite still. It was true, then. She was receiving *two* signals.

It was unknown in the history of Zaran, but there it was. When she had said there was only one option, she had assumed that she would tune only to Kirk. There had been that affinity between them from the first moments in the clearing—the beginning of an imprinting which would deepen as choice became irrevocable until it was a band of force between them.

She had fought it, but it was not to be fought. She had even set the Vulcan against it. He had not known that it was not merely *his* need which she answered.

But that should merely have made it impossible to bond with either. To have this awareness of both was also not dreamed of in Zaran philosophy. But then, as Kirk had said of Spock, neither was *she*. Nor were they all.

She lifted her head and tried to sense which direction belonged to which. She found she could not be certain. The call was virtually equal. And the pull was in opposite directions. The Master of Totality had known how to turn the screws tightly.

"Spock!" she called silently. It was doubtful that the thin thread of connection would carry a mental message across distance, yet. But it was necessary to try.

She received no answer. But from one of the directions it was as if she sensed dimly some massive resistance. She knew then. It was one of the two men—sensing her also dimly and warning her to go after the other.

With some effort she turned away from it, to the opposite direction, and moved. It had to be the Vulcan who would send that message. And she firmly turned her back on him and went for Kirk.

There had always been only one option in that sense, too. The Vulcan was far better equipped to survive here unarmed. He was vastly stronger and raised to survive on a planet which could rival this one for danger. He would have survived Vulcan in the Kaswan trial—at the age of seven.

Kirk was a Starship Captain. What training and sheer wiliness and courage could do, he would do. But he was Human, and all of Starfleet's survival training was not equal to unaided Human survival here. Even her people would not survive long unarmed. Nor, for that matter, would the Vulcan. And only she was armed.

The only chance to save both men lay in a single direction. She moved quickly through the lower terrace. . . .

Chapter 20

Kirk found a small stand of what looked like blue bamboo. The shafts were long and straight and tapered toward the tip. He put his back against a tree and worried at one of the shafts until he was able to snap it at a joint across a rock. He hefted it experimentally. The ten-foot length would make a serviceable spear.

He would have preferred a cannon. There was nothing here which he wanted to touch with a ten-foot spear. And most of the local fauna looked capable of using it for a toothpick.

He picked out a short length which might be stabbed like a knife and tucked it into the robe belt. The stuff was too rigid to make a good bow, he decided, and he doubted he would have the leisure. He heard the coughing of the cat behind him still.

And this time he looked up again at the low branches where they had first found Sola. All right. She knew this territory. He doubted that the trees would help him against the cat, but they might keep down the werewolves and a few other things. He found a couple of low branches and swung up into them. Many were wide enough to stand on easily and from most he could reach some other interlocking branch before it narrowed to become a tightrope.

He brightened a little. Things were looking up. What worried him was that Sola and Spock would be frantically combing the planet for him. Or perhaps the Totality would have given her some place to start, and she, or they, would be down here, beating the bushes for him. Mate-hunt? Would she come for him if that were the only way she could come? There was, he realized, another danger. Perhaps the Totality did not merely wish to have her hunt him, but wanted to reduce him to some state where Totality would seem like a refuge. In which case the Totality was probably hunting him, too. . . .

He turned to look at his back-trail and found a saber-toothed black cat-bear, for want of a better description, looking at him from a branch twenty feet away. The cat-bear was about a dozen feet long. . . .

Spock moved through the upper terrace with a Vulcan concentration which excluded all else save the vine or balance-branch which he needed for the next forward progress. It was not unlike a balance skill taught to Vulcan children in infant school. The children were not, however, required to practice it some 20.3 meters above the jungle floor.

But there were no obstructions here. He had attempted the lower terrace of wide interlocking branches. It was safer, but the need to detour around various interlocked areas did not suit his need for haste. The ground, of course, was quite impossible. Therefore, he reached back into ancient skills once learned as play and adapted them to an alien environment. At this height he could often vault on a tall, thin sapling for ten or twenty meters. Speed was of the essence.

He was not certain what guide he was following. It was some directional sense which could span distance, but he was not certain whether it led to Sola, or whether it was the still more primitive sense which had once or twice led him to Kirk.

In either case he was certain that it would ultimately lead him to both of them. Sola would, of course, in all logic, go after Kirk—or she would have to answer to Spock. She would know that.

But huntress that she was, she could not be expected to cope with the trap which Spock expected the Totality to lay for them.

Wherefore the Vulcan hurled himself through the trees like a projectile, and there was little in him of Vulcan's thousand years of peace or of the disciplined Starfleet officer. This was jungle and desert, a million years old, and Spock of Vulcan and all his savage ancestors were at home here.

If he did not reach Sola and Kirk in time, this was where he would die. . . .

Chapter 21

McCoy turned on Gailbraith. He had brought the Ambassador to his own home turf, Sickbay, and now he meant to have an answer.

"Ambassador," he said, "I'm not sure how much soul I own, and you are just about the last buyer I would sell it to. But I consider that I am now left in effective command of this ship. I cannot know whether Mr. Scott or any other crew member is free of either the Totality or your Oneness and therefore fit to command. I don't know what you did to Jim Kirk in that link Spock pulled him out of. I don't like what you have evidently cooked up with the Totality. But I have to hold this ship together and find its Captain and First Officer. And Sola. If your price is my soul, I will make you the same offer the Captain made. If he joins you, I will, too. But you must leave me clear until that time and help me to hold the ship and to find them."

Gailbraith smiled. "That is rather a hard bargain, Doctor—considering that if I get your Captain's soul, I would almost certainly get yours, too."

McCoy faced him flatly. "Gailbraith, you don't hold all the cards. Under Code Seven as Senior Medical Officer I am empowered to take certain steps—including, if necessary, a destruct sequence. And even if you could get your people off, your Oneness could not survive on that planet, either. I suggest you accept my bargain."

McCoy did not describe the limits of his power or the depth of his reluctance to use it. He had played poker from Georgia to Jim Kirk.

Gailbraith smiled. "Doctor, you will never know whether it is to my immediate purpose to assist you, or whether I merely pretend to do so while waiting to take you off guard. However, within those limits—and in my own time—I will assist you for that price."

McCoy took a deep breath. He wasn't certain what you were supposed to do after you sold your soul to the Devil. But he had better get on with it.

"You will keep Mr. Scott and the command crew free of the Totality and your Oneness," he began. "Scott, Sulu, Uhura, Chekov, Chapel, a few others I'll name."

Gailbraith shook his head. "Three of those already belong to the Totality, or to me."

McCoy felt his heart contract as if in a vise. Scotty? Chapel? Any of them. Dear God. Then, in fact, he *was* holding the fort, the last line of defense.

"You will tell me which ones," he said. "And then you will help me find the Captain."

Gailbraith shrugged. "Possibly. In my time."

Kirk backed warily along a branch, holding the cat-bear with his eyes, feeling his way with feet and one hand, until he backed up against the trunk of a life-tree.

He braced the spear against the trunk, but he did not expect it to help him much. Even if it impaled the cat-bear, he would probably be crushed by the great beast's weight and killed in its death-throes.

But it was the first rule of survival that you kept trying until you were already dead—and for some time after that.

The cat-bear looked at him as if at a rather interesting morsel, then charged.

He braced the spear, and as the point took the animal in the chest, he jumped. He was perhaps twenty feet off the ground, but he broke the fall slightly by grabbing at a branch or two on the way down.

He landed, hard, and rolled, and then the animal landed beside him, a snarling, spitting mass of claws and teeth, dying.

He scrambled away and backed up until he was trapped by the trunks of life-trees. He held the feeble short length of blue bamboo like a knife and waited while the animal towered up like a bear on two legs, twice his height.

Then as it reached him, it crumpled and he barely escaped its collapsing weight. He was surprised to find it dead at his feet.

He turned away, somehow shocked by the death of so large and beautiful a thing, and yet surprised to be alive.

He would not survive many more such encounters. And somewhere he had smashed the previously injured arm against a branch and knew that Gailbraith's healing was not perfect. It had restored the essential function, but not the bone-deep healthy strength. He was in pain again, and he felt the deep shock lying in wait for him. One ankle was sprained, and he doubted that he could make it in the trees now.

He moved out on the ground, limping, looking for more of the scarce blue bamboo. An unarmed man could not last long on the ground, but he must find another weapon, and he must keep going.

Somehow what disturbed him most was the thought of Sola, or Spock, finding his body under some cat-bear or werewolf.

Or—not finding it . . .

Chapter 22

Kirk found no more blue bamboo, but he picked up a hefty length of something like ironwood which might do as a serviceable club.

The jungle opened out suddenly into a wide clearing and above the trees on the other side he saw the top of a mountain. Spock's words came back to him: "Camouflaged power and intelligent life-form readings in a solitary volcano near the clearing where Sola landed."

Suddenly things made a little more sense. The Totality would be testing them all on more than one level. Soljenov would put Kirk down within range of a determined assault on his own fortress, to see if Kirk would take up the gauntlet—or take the bait.

He couldn't know Kirk very well, after all, if he had to ask the question. Or then again, perhaps he did know Kirk very well, and it was a sophisticated version of "Won't you come into my parlor?"

In any case, Kirk fixed the direction by the sun and plunged into the jungle in the direction of the mountain. He would take bearding the enemy in his den, any day, over wandering aimlessly in a jungle trying to avoid becoming dinner—or waiting to be rescued.

And, in truth, he could not wait. It was coming to him that he could not allow Sola to find him. Under conditions of mate-hunt she would doubtless have no choice but to mate, perhaps also to bond. And he could not allow himself that. There was Spock.

In fact, it was coming to him that there *was no* solution to that. He could not see the Vulcan make this effort to break free—only to slam him back into his chains.

No.

And at the same time, he could not change the fact that he would always be there as a threat to both of them. He could not leave. He could not deny the lightning which had struck him, too. Even if he said nothing, did nothing, he doubted that Sola could deny it indefinitely.

If she found him here, he doubted that she could deny it at all.

Some dim thought was coming to him of a radical solution to that and other problems. But he could not quite bring it into focus, yet. He knew that it had something to do with what he had experienced with Gailbraith in that brief encounter with Oneness. He could not fully remember it all, and he knew that his mind, or Gailbraith's, was blocking the remembrance. But he knew that the pull of Oneness had been strong. It was shockingly *different*—and yet he had lived his life exploring the different. There in the Oneness what was forbidden became the normal, and there was no more solitude or secret or separation.

There he could perhaps endure alone the separation which would have to come if the other two were to be free.

And suppose that instead of exploring Gailbraith's One, he went into Soljenov's Totality?

If the Totality could not be made to abandon conquest from without—maybe he could stop it from within?

Apparently he had become a major objective of both

superentities, Gailbraith's and Soljenov's. And maybe something could be made out of that. Such as a lot of trouble . . .

He increased his pace toward the mountain.

And then something reached down from a tree and closed steely coils around him—coils as thick as his thigh.

He looked up to see what might as well have been a dragon—a fanged head on a thin neck, thick body, and a tail the size of a large python, which had wrapped around him.

He tried to get his club arm free, but it was hopeless. He was being drawn up toward the fangs. He thought that he screamed, mentally, to anyone who could hear. But he expected no answer . . .

Sola heard the scream of her mate.

There was no sound, but there was now the link between them which made him her life. She moved, and there was little left of the Free Agent of the Federation. She was the Zaran female, answering the cry of her mate across a million-year-old jungle.

She flew now, taking risks she would not have taken before, hurling herself across large open spaces to catch precarious handholds, then swinging up again to run along tightrope-thin branches or vault on the thin saplings.

And still she was certain that she would be too late.

She sent out the psionic hunting cry of the Zaran female—and now it had the power of a female in mate-hunt. It was a warning which could strike terror to the heart of prey or predator, and it might give some predator pause, just long enough.

Then she was there, and she saw Kirk crushed in the coils of a tree-serpent. He was all but unconscious, and the serpent's head was looking into his face. It had perhaps been stopped from crushing the life completely out of him, or using its poison fangs, by her cry.

She leaped across the last twenty feet to land on the serpent's woven bower. It was semi-intelligent and wove nests for itself, often in front of great tree-caves which were its lair.

She could not use the phaser. It would hit Kirk, too. And a stun heavy enough to stop the serpent might kill him. She lashed out with her wrist-coil, wrapping the energy coil around the serpent's throat just below the head and jerking the fanged head away from Kirk's face. The coil was not heavy enough to stun the serpent, but it made the beast pay attention.

It turned and came after her, dragging Kirk still in its tail. She made the coil flicker, striking it again, reaching for the vulnerable spot where the coil would have enough power to stun the small, active brain.

The fanged head struck at her, and she stepped inside it, threw herself on the neck, and finally reached a vulnerable spot behind the ear with her wrist-weapon at point-blank range.

The serpent began to collapse, stunned, and she saw that it would fall off the edge of the bower—taking Kirk with it.

She leaped to pull him out of the relaxing coils of the tail. The serpent poured limply over the edge of the bower, and she heard the thud from below before she was quite certain that she had managed to hold Kirk with the strength of necessity.

The serpent would doubtless recover in an hour or so. She would not.

Kirt was semiconscious. She half-carried, half-guided him into the serpent's tree-cave. It was clean and quiet, and no other predator would come here.

She started to go over Kirk. The thin Sickbay outfit was in tatters. She found a scratch on a shoulder, not from the serpent but from his fight with the *cranth*. She had found the great animal which he would see as cat and bear. She saw his makeshift spear, and she did not know yet how he had survived.

He was conscious now, and he looked up at her with a faint smile. "So much for my theory," he said. "Thank you."

Her own voice was strained and low in her throat. "What theory?"

"I didn't want you to find me. At least, I didn't want to want it." He reached out and took her hand. "Sola, what I said on the ship still has to go for us. We can't give Spock back to the chains and the vultures. And now we can't give the Totality what it wants, either."

"Spock sent me back to *you*," she said. "He is stronger even than you know, and he will not be harmed by this. As for what the Totality wants, it may have overplayed its hand just now in setting one of you against the other. If I can keep some balance, perhaps I can stop short of bonding."

He frowned then. "Is that safe for you?"

She laughed low in her throat. "No. But it is safer than the alternative."

She leaned away from him and started to stand up. She was not certain whether or how long she could keep going without the ending which was necessary to the mate-hunt. But she could not trust herself to stop short of the bonding. And she would not override his resistance with the threat to her life.

He caught her wrist again and stopped her from moving. "What you are not saying," he said, "is that it is almost what it was for Spock. It is your life—isn't it?"

"No," she lied.

But he reached up to catch her shoulder and pulled her down. "Your mistake," he said. "Did you suppose either one of us would allow *that?*"

Then his lips found hers, and she knew that he was right, whatever danger or impossibility it might lead to, there was no way, even, that she could find Spock until she had finished with this—if it could be finished. This moment, at least, was theirs, and must be. . . .

Chapter 23

Spock seemed to have lost the fragile thread of direction he had been following. Perhaps something had disturbed it. He had sensed a kind of turbulence in the tenuous sense of presence which he had followed—danger, close brushes with death. Then there was some interruption toward the end which he could not read, some peculiar intensity of emotion. . . .

Now he stopped, having no guide except the previous direction. He could no longer be certain that he was not hurling himself away from his own quarry. From one of them—or both of them . . .

He stayed for a moment in the fork of a great tree, questing, thinking. Then he set off, altering his course slightly and redoubling his pace.

He had been aware for some time from his height in the trees of the volcanic crater which loomed ahead and slightly to his right. It was in the general direction of the last trace of directional awareness he had had.

But more than that, he knew the man who was his Captain. If he lived, Kirk would sooner or later catch a glimpse of the volcano, and when he did, he would head for it. The mathematical probability approached certainty.

Kirk would storm any citadel rather than move without purpose. And Spock knew from previous sensor analysis that this geo-thermal-powered citadel was essentially impregnable and quite probably a layer-on-layer trap aimed precisely at them.

Sola would doubtless have some idea of that danger. But if she found Kirk first—or if she already *had*—she would undoubtedly consider joining him in the assault. That was, of course, assuming that she was in any condition to do so.

Spock had been gratified to sense that she had yielded to the logic of the situation and pursued the mate-hunt after Kirk. She would have known that Spock would accept no other solution.

But he was quite certain that there was also a danger for her in any form of mate-hunt. And his earlier weakness—or perhaps even his strength—might well have condemned her to a danger he did not know. Kirk had sent her back to him, once. If he attempted to do so here, the results might be catastrophic, possibly even fatal for her. And if he did not . . .

If he did *not,* Kirk would almost certainly become bonded to her, irrevocably. That would unleash her powers to make her the Totality's weapon. And Kirk would become the hostage to fortune which the Totality would use to control Sola.

In that event there was virtually zero probability that Spock would ever see either of them again.

Spock moved down into the lower terrace of branches, sensing that he was close enough that he might pick up some actual trail or trace. He had better arrive first. Intercept Sola. Interrupt. She would be much less vulnerable to the use of Spock as a hostage, and he was better equipped to survive the Totality.

He moved with more care, not wanting some hazard to

claim him now. Fortunately as a Vulcan he was even reasonably well-equipped to survive here.

Spock stopped. On the jungle floor below he saw the body of some large animal. It looked as if it had been stopped by a blue spear. He half-climbed, half-dropped down to it—a fairly easy matter in the less-than-Vulcan gravity.

The spear was a length of crude bamboolike fibrous growth, and he knew who would have used it.

Spock turned at a sound behind him and found himself facing a very large erect, manlike creature—covered in glossy black silver-tipped hair. It was half-again his height and six times his weight. And by the tooth structure, which was bared at him, it was carnivorous.

It appeared to be a semi-intelligent local equivalent of a large anthropoid, perhaps similar to Earth's legendary Bigfoot, but with overtones here of saber-toothed cave-bear.

Spock considered that it was in all probability gregarious and also hunted in packs.

He had possibly been somewhat hasty in assessing his capacity to survive here, Spock decided.

Then the man-thing attacked him.

Kirk pulled away from Sola with a sudden sense of acute unease—danger, some urgent warning . . .

Suddenly he saw the same sense in her eyes.

He had noticed the communicator she had. "Call the ship," he said. "Make sure Spock hasn't beamed down."

She shook her head. "The communicator does not work here. But also—Spock was beamed down a moment after you were—to offer me a choice."

He was suddenly on his feet. "Then he's out *there!*"

She moved for the door. "I stood no chance of finding him, once committed to you. He will have been on our trail."

"You should have gone after *him,*" he said.

She merely looked at him, and he saw what the choice had cost her—and that the interruption now might cost her life. "Stay here," she said, and was suddenly off through the trees.

He knew she was probably right in telling him to stay put. He was not in the best shape, and he was too slow in the trees. He could too easily get lost or fall afoul of some other predator.

But he had some sense that Spock was in mortal danger.

She had left him the phaser on her weapon belt in the cave. He reached in and got it.

But he knew that all of that was largely rationalization. He would have gone bare-handed.

He moved off through the trees, trying to follow her vanishing form or, at least, her direction—although he had some sense that he could find the action himself.

Something had aimed him like an arrow . . .

Sola arrived in time to see Spock drop one of the silver-tipped man-hunters with a Vulcan nerve-pinch.

He was locked in the embrace with a force which had been close to snapping even a Vulcan spine before he could reach the nerve-hold. The manling fell as if axed.

But its band came out of the underbrush and began to close on the Vulcan.

He put his foot on the body of the fallen male and tried Sola's trick of projecting a psionic message of triumph and strength—a kind of primitive I-am-Spock, I-rule-here.

The manling band stopped. Then one of the young males stepped out and prepared to close with the Vulcan. The young male's challenge was at least superior to the alternative —a mass attack by the band. If Spock could close with them one at a time, he might at least delay the outcome.

However, he could not conceivably win against the faster, stronger young manling.

She saw—and sensed psionically—that no fiber of Spock's being, no scent, no psionic aura, acknowledged the possibility of defeat.

That in itself was a powerful deterrent. The young male hesitated. Sola waited. There was the faintest chance, slim but conceivable, that the manling would be bluffed out and withdraw. Their dawn-age minds should not be able to confront this confident, apparently fearless prime male from another world. Some things cut across species and even world-lines.

Her single wrist-coil was not a sufficient weapon against a concerted attack by this large band.

Then one of the younger males jeered, urging the challenging male on—in their prelingual word-sounds, questioning the young male's courage and his maleness.

The challenging male flung back an insult at the jeerers and

charged Spock. The Vulcan met the charge, vaulting past the
bull-manling to try to get on its back. But it was quick and
young, with advantage of height, weight, reach. It caught him
out of the air with one swipe of a long hand-paw and sent him
reeling to slam against a tree.

Then Sola leaped down in front of Spock into the center of
the manling band. That changed the nature of the conflict
from male-clash to hunt-of-eating-enemy. An older female
moved toward her first, then they all started to close in.

"Get out of here," Spock snarled.

But she flicked out with the wrist-coil to stun the young
male closing on Spock, then the old female. The female
collapsed against her, almost taking her down.

Then the band made a concerted charge, and she was
trying to pick them off with the coil. She could feel Spock at
her back, fending off attackers with hands, feet, nerve-
pinches.

For a moment she wished she had brought the phaser, but
she could not leave Kirk unarmed, nor let him come.

Then she heard something from the trees and saw Kirk
standing on a branch, trying to fire the phaser. Apparently
they were to be permitted only one weapon. The phaser did
not fire.

"Stay back!" she shouted to Kirk.

She felt the Vulcan turn, see Kirk, and say, "Stop!"

But it.was already too late. Kirk had brought his ironwood
club and with it he dropped down into the middle of the fray
and threw himself between an animal and Sola. The club was
a hopelessly inadequate weapon against the great manlings.
But he waded in as if he did not know that, or care.

She found the wrist-coil flickering with an inspired precision which she could never have summoned by an effort of
will. It wove a sudden net of protection around her vulnerable, insufferably brave chosen-mate-to-be. Or was it around
both of her choices? For she felt now again the pull of Spock.

In either case the manlings suddenly sensed some terrible
unity among the three strange beings. The first strange-male
redoubled his efforts and locked his hands together to chop
with clubbed hands. The smaller male scored with his club on
vulnerable spots. The strange-female was possessed.

The manlings turned suddenly, dragging their wounded,
their stunned, away with them.

After a long moment the clearing was quiet. Three figures still stood in the center of it. Then two of them turned on the other one.

"I told you to stay at the tree-cave," Sola said.

"And *I*," Spock added, "to stay out of this fight."

Kirk sighed and looked considerably the worse for wear, but unrepentant. He could not quite repress a grin at the sight of Spock, alive.

"So—sue me," he said.

Sola saw the Vulcan severely tempted to some less civilized form of dealing with that particular illogic. Or perhaps she merely projected her own temptation.

"You could have been killed, twice over, on your way here," she said. "But there might have been some small excuse for coming with the phaser. There was *none* for jumping down when it failed to fire. At best you gave us more to protect—and more to distract us. You are far more vulnerable than a Vulcan, untrained for this, and armed only with a twig which a juvenile manling could take away from you."

He sobered and looked at her squarely. "That's quite true. And could I have failed to do it? What would you then expect me to do with the rest of my life?" He smiled then. "Besides, you may have noticed that you did such a job of protecting me that you won."

For once she was silent. She had noticed it. And she had noticed that his illogic should have made her turn toward the Vulcan's welcome sanity. In fact, it did. But she was surprised to notice that there was also some powerful element in her which loved that quality in the Human, however dangerous or illogical it was. There was some deep, primitive response to the male who would throw himself between his mate and the predator. It was not a survival characteristic—for the male. But it was for his mate and his seed . . .

Chapter 24

Spock noted that there was some different footing between the other two, but he was unable to determine its exact nature.

His conjecture did not square with the wound-tight tension he sensed in Sola. Unless his danger had interrupted something.

"I recommend we adjourn from the immediate vicinity," he said. There were still stirrings in the underbrush, and the stun effect of the wrist-weapon was of uncertain duration.

"Agreed, Mr. Spock," Kirk said, and looked somewhat dubiously at the trees, which offered no easy route of ingress for him at the moment. There were one or two climbs which might be attempted by an active Vulcan or a trained Zaran.

Spock noted that although Kirk had come by the trees, he walked with a limp, which would make every step a hazard.

Sola was inspecting the terrain with the same eye. "Ground travel is impossible. Every predator within scent or hearing of our three separate battles will be converging on this area. And in moments the light will fail, and we cannot travel at all—certainly at least not until moonrise. We must reach a place of safety."

"Where?" Kirk asked.

"Where we were," she said, and Spock saw the Human look a little startled.

"*There?*" he said.

"The tree-serpent, on Zaran, at least, ordinarily does not return to a tree-cave it has lost. Nor do other predators usually approach it. Anything which has defeated a tree-dragon is presumed formidable."

Spock took a look at his particular Human St. George, somewhat bedraggled now, and tried to visualize that Human's historic encounter with a dragon which even other predators here would respect.

Kirk shook his head. "It wasn't *me,* Mr. Spock. *She* was—formidable."

Spock indicated the dead feline-ursine creature which had encountered the blue bamboo. "That also was not your handiwork?"

Kirk shrugged an admission. "Necessity is a mother, Mr. Spock. Let's go." He indicated a leg up for Spock to a likely climb to the trees. But Spock was able to jump to catch a handhold and in a moment he was up and leaning down to pull the Human up. Sola covered them from the ground, then also jumped to accept a lift from Spock.

For a moment as he lifted her their eyes met, and he was surprised to sense that there was no wall between them, no silencing of the carrier-hum of communication which had started to form between them. Was it possible, then, that there had been no bonding? But in that event, he must still fear for her life.

He put the question aside as they moved off. Sola led, picking footing which would be as safe as possible for Kirk with his injured ankle. Spock covered the rear, staying close enough for a quick lunge if the ankle gave way.

Kirk set his teeth and moved.

Before they reached their objective the sudden tropic night had fallen, becoming black as moonless Vulcan. Here the thick jungle even obscured the starlight.

Sola dropped back to guide Kirk step by step now. To the Human it must have been as black as the inside of a sealed chamber. The Zaran woman must have retained some slight vision. Spock managed.

Then Sola stopped. For the first time she risked using the coil of energy from the wrist-weapon as a light. It flared briefly and lit a woven bower of branches and a large cave in the huge trunk of a life-tree. Both were empty.

There was a roar on the ground. Spock looked down to see an unmistakable dragon, large, not to be compared to the dragons of Berengaria.

Its thick tail alone was the size of a Terran anaconda, perhaps twenty-five feet long. Its neck was almost equally long. It could have reached them in the trees.

Spock braced for attack, but Sola sent another flare of the wrist weapon in its direction, not touching it. But it had evidently learned its lesson and recoiled, hissing disconsolately. The hissing was perhaps digestive gas, and Spock saw suddenly the crackle from the dragon's mouth of an electrical charge, perhaps like the electrical eels of Earth, or the great eel-birds of Regulus.

The gas caught fire and shot up toward them like a flamethrower. Spock made a move to cover the other two, but Sola snapped out with the wrist-coil again as she dodged the flame.

The flame stopped. Spock turned in the light of small burning branches to see the fire-dragon shake its great head and turn away. Spock moved out and snapped off the dry, burning branches of the bower, brought them back to the mouth of the cave, and found a ledge of living wood damp with sap, which would not soon burn. On it he laid the burning branches out to form a small campfire.

"It would appear our position has already been advertised sufficiently," he said. "I see no harm in a fire, and it may offer some protection."

There was a certain primitive satisfaction in sharing a fire after the dangers met and shared. And he saw an appreciation of that in the eyes of the other two as he tamed and brought the fire.

But this was not a fire Spock could share. It was clear enough to him that Sola had made her choice and that Kirk had accepted it. The chance of an interruption by danger could not be an argument. And to impose his presence might well cost her life. Spock sensed the unresolved tension mounting toward physiological overload.

He reached in and picked up the useless phaser Kirk had brought back. "If you will excuse me," Spock said, "I will see to the phaser and stand watch."

He turned without allowing a reply and moved rather stiffly to the far corner of the fire-dragon's bower, taking a torch with him and propping it as a solitary fire and light. He started to look at the phaser, focusing all his concentration on that, ignoring low voices in the tree-cave.

After a few moments he heard footsteps behind him. He didn't look, but he knew who it was.

"You wouldn't be 'going off into the night,' Mr. Spock?"

Spock looked up as Kirk sat down beside him. "I am attempting to repair a phaser and to stand watch. I expect to be some time."

"Spock," Kirk said, "she came after me because I didn't stand a snowball's chance. She counted on you to survive."

Spock shrugged. "That was the only logical choice," he said, "as I attempted to convey to her. However, the reason of choice does not alter the choice." He looked at Kirk. "Not for her, not for you. Nor would I change it. Go to her now."

Kirk shook his head.

"Jim," Spock said, "I once told you that the woman you loved, Edith Keeler, had to die—for the fate of the galaxy. I saw no other solution, but it was you who had to live with the decision, and the loss. I will not see you lose again."

Kirk was silent for a long moment. "You know, then. Or you've guessed. At least—*I* guessed when she found me, that it was her life, too. That's why—"

"You need not explain."

"I'll decide what I need, damn it! And right now I need you to come back in that cave and fight for her. I may pin your elegant Vulcan ears back, later, if I'm up to it. But I won't be chosen because I'm the one to be rescued, or because the Totality has pulled some string."

"You were chosen, from the beginning," Spock said.

Kirk shrugged. "She didn't know *you*. Spock, she's in

danger, and if I thought I was the only way to save her, which I did, I *would*. But I don't think it would work now. She sensed—even then—that you were in trouble."

"It proves nothing."

"Logic, Spock. If we dance to the tune the Totality called, if I bond with her—or even if you did—they would control her. Spock, is there some possible salvation in the fact that we three—*are* three?"

Spock looked at him carefully. "Unknown, Captain. Insufficient data."

Kirk reached out and handed Spock the communicator. "I suppose it's asking too much that you get this back in working order?"

Spock inspected it, rising to the bait. "Considering that we lack even stone knives and bear claws, this time, possibly."

Kirk grinned. "I'm afraid I'm always asking too much of you, Mr. Spock. Now come back into the cave."

Spock rose without a word and obeyed.

Chapter 25

Kirk watched the Vulcan work, as he had on so many other missions, the intent face bent over the fine work . . . "I am attempting to construct a mnemonic circuit using stone knives and bear claws," Spock had told Edith Keeler.

Now again there was the argument from the necessity of the galaxy. Kirk was perhaps more tired than he knew of the necessity of the galaxy. Today he had felt the pull of the bonding, strong and sweet, more than the flesh, and not forbidden to him this time by some gulf which could never be bridged. This woman belonged in his world and time, lived on his terms, played in his league as a Free Agent.

Their joining would make her give a hostage to fortune whom she could not lose, would doubtless put them both at

the mercy of the Totality. It might well loose her powers in
some way which would unleash Oneness on the galaxy. But at
one moment Kirk had almost been prepared to risk that, and
he sensed that her resistance on that count had also been
stretched to the point of the unendurable. Even now he saw
in her fire-lit face that the pull of the bonding was strong. She
might have risked all the other hazards.

It had been a more personal consideration which had truly
held them back until interruption saved them from having to
admit that there was one unalterable objection. That objection had a name, and the name was Spock.

"Spock?" Kirk said.

The Vulcan looked up and met his eyes, and Kirk saw that
the Vulcan had missed nothing in the tree-cave, Kirk's
tattered Sickbay jacket left behind, and Sola's belt. The
Vulcan's eyes held no accusation, merely comprehension.

"The Totality," Kirk said carefully, "has assumed that the
necessary conclusion of mate-hunt could not be resisted or
deferred, and that it must inevitably lead to bonding. That
was a mistake."

"Indeed?" Spock said, as if they were talking about a point
of scientific curiosity.

"Indeed," he said firmly. "Mistake number two. Soljenov
assumed he could force her to choose. He could not. There
were practical reasons why she would necessarily come after
me, if she wanted to preserve us both."

"That was," Spock said, "a message which I attempted to
convey."

Sola lifted her head. "Your message came through, Spock.
Very clearly. I could not have gone to you with his body."
She met the Vulcan's eyes. "Nor he to you, with mine. That
would have been his only choice."

"So I surmised," the Vulcan said.

"You *surmised!*" Kirk said, startled.

Spock shrugged fractionally. "One cannot stir such physiological and psionic processes to such a peak and offer no
completion without grave, perhaps fatal, risk." He turned to
look at Sola. "Even now, if you have evaded the final
necessity of bonding, I suspect you are at risk."

"If I am, I must be," she said. "I cannot choose. Today
when I was called to hunt—I was called in two directions. I
still am."

Spock was silent for a long moment. Finally he nodded. "It is something I had wanted to know."

So did I, Kirk thought, but he did not voice it. From somewhere the plan which had been coming to him in bits and pieces began to fit together. It would not have worked, not even for Spock, if she had felt no such call. And Kirk had thought once that afternoon that perhaps she had not.

At some primitive level he felt a sudden, blinding wish that she had not. Then he pulled himself back to what had to be his main focus.

"Spock, what I said today, to both of you, still goes." He started to move out of the mouth of the cave. "I'll take the first watch."

Spock's arm blocked the way. "I am neither fragile nor in need of assistance. Nor will you move beyond the portal."

Kirk looked at him in some astonishment. He could not remember when, if ever, the Vulcan had spoken to him in that tone.

"Nor am *I,*" Sola said, and he perceived that he was in some difficulty with both of them.

"For the record," he said rather flatly, "neither am *I.*" He gave a moment's thought to trying to move beyond the Vulcan's arm, thought better of it. "Mr. Spock," he said in the command tone, "about that communicator . . . ?"

Spock hefted it in his other hand. "It is in perfect order, Captain, and I suspect that it always was. If we cannot now reach the *Enterprise,* and I detect no blocking force-field, we must conclude that the *Enterprise*—or at least its communications network—is in enemy hands."

Spock hit the control on the communicator at Kirk's nod. "Spock to *Enterprise.* Come in please."

There was no answer. Spock consulted a reading. "There is no force-field. The *Enterprise* does not answer—because it cannot."

Kirk looked restlessly at the cave entrance. They had his ship! The heart of it, at least. And he was helpless here. These two would certainly not let him get away by himself, even if he were to convince himself that it was anything short of suicide to try that.

"How long to moonrise?" he asked Sola.

It was Spock who answered. "Approximately two-point-one-three hours."

Sola moved toward the mouth of the cave. "I brought one force-field generator. If it works, no watch is needed."

She set the control and in fact a force-field sprang up to flicker across the entrance, blocking any animal or humanoid danger. It was better than a thorn boma.

"All right," Kirk said. "We'll rest for two hours. It will pay in the long run." He himself felt ready to drop. The other two did not seem much the worse for wear, but each of them had been very close to death this day. He suspected that Sola still was. And they would all probably be much closer to it still before the night was over.

"I see no alternative," Kirk said, "to a direct assault on the crater. The Totality has some interest in us. Soljenov will quite possibly even let us in."

In fact, Kirk was certain that it was he, chiefly, whom the force in the mountain wanted, and if he came close enough, he expected it to take him. Then he would make his bargain for a galaxy—and two souls . . .

Meanwhile the three of them had reached a peculiar resting-place here, and there was an odd kind of comfort in the presence of the other two, even for these brief hours. He settled down to try to rest.

Chapter 26

Captain's Log, Enterprise, Supplementary. Chief Engineer Montgomery Scott in temporary command. Captain Kirk and First Officer Spock, together with the Zaran—ah —passenger, Sola Thane, remain missing. Communications reports no contact, in spite of the fact that Sola Thane was equipped with a working communicator. Sensor scans of the planet below are unable to distinguish their life-form readings from the extremely high level of background biological activity.

We are no closer to any means of detecting or combatting the takeover of Enterprise crew by either the Zaran Totality or Ambassador Gailbraith's Oneness. Personally, I am not a' that sure which is worse.

I myself believe that I remain clear of both of them, but

I am certain of no one else. Perhaps not even of myself. Doctor McCoy believes that there is a latency period in which even the victim does not know or remember that he or she has been taken over. Victims continue to think and act as before, but their actions may unconsciously serve the Totality, or they may blank out for a moment something they are made to do.

If that is true, it may be that I command a ship of aliens who wear all the familiar faces of family.

McCoy came onto the Bridge to hear the last of Scott's log dictation. He saw the Scot turn toward him with the slight, guarded speculation which said: Are you One of them?

Then Scott nodded to him. "Any progress?" he asked. McCoy noted that Scott did not even use his name.

McCoy shook his head. "That's right, Scotty. I may be One. Or you may. Meanwhile, I think I may have bought us both some time. Anything on Jim? Spock? Her?" He saw Scott's negative. "Or about the Totality stronghold?"

Scott sighed. "It's a sweet piece of engineering. Short of blowing up the planet—or at least touching off an active volcano, I'd say it's impregnable—"

"What if you touched off the volcano?"

Scott shrugged. "For all we know the Captain is sitting on top of it. Or—in it. I'd say the Totality would have an auxiliary escape mechanism. Transport capability—and likely a ship. And if we attack, they'd more than likely be all over our Bridge the next moment—if they aren't already." He turned to look around the Bridge. Uhura sat at communications, looking darkly beautiful, as always. But was she One? Communications would be a prime target.

McCoy looked at Scott, who might also be One. "Scotty," he said deliberately, "I'm going down. If those three—or any of them—are alive down there, I think they'll sooner or later turn up at that volcano. That may be what this test is all about. But God knows what kind of condition they'll be in. I'm not going to miss this."

"And just what do y' count on to keep *you* alive, Doctor?"

McCoy looked him in the eye. "I'm taking Gailbraith. And Mr. Dobius."

"*What?*" Scott said. "But Gailbraith is just as likely to glom you for the Oneness as look at you. And you *know* Dobius has been taken by Gailbraith *and* the Totality. Though just how they expect him to think with two heads I dinna ken."

"That's the point, Scotty. He's the only one I can be fairly sure isn't *totally* controlled by the Totality. So long as he's controlled by himself or by Gailbraith, I'm all right. And if we need to contact the Totality, it can probably be through him. Besides, he's the strongest candidate to survive down there."

"I do na' like it, Leonard," Scott said.

McCoy grimaced. "Neither do *I*, Scotty. But I have to go. And I can't let you stop me, even if I wanted to. *You* could be controlled."

"Aye."

"Don't worry about *me*, Mr. Scott," McCoy said. "By Gailbraith's calculations, in less than two hours the Totality should have total control of the *Enterprise*."

"Doctor," Scott said, "over my body."

"*That*," McCoy growled, "is what I'm afraid of."

Chapter 27

By moonlight they traveled through the trees. The moon, nearly full and more than twice the apparent size of Earth's moon, cast a respectable blue-white glow. Many of the trees and flowers also fluoresced blue-white in the moonlight, lighting their way as if they walked in a diamond night.

And ahead was the ominous, red-gold glow of the living crater.

Both were spectacularly beautiful and dangerous. In the jungle great tree-orchids opened glowing blooms the size of a man. Somewhere else they would see tiny, perfect blooms the size of a fingernail—scattered by millions.

Nor was it all innocence. Kirk saw what he was certain was the local equivalent of a Venus's-flytrap. But this plant was of a size to trap cat-bear or man. He had almost walked into its open jaws before Sola caught him and steered him aside.

"This is like your home?" he asked.

She laughed. "Like the wild areas, yes. We have created certain parklike areas where children may learn in safety. But as on Vulcan there is no real safety except in knowledge learned very early."

He had a picture of her as a very small girl, moving in these hazards—and he turned for a moment to see that Spock must be having much the same thought. Possibly the Vulcan, who had survived the Kaswan at age seven, would understand that girl better than he did.

But then, Kirk also understood the woman who was the Free Agent only too well.

For this moment they all moved suspended in time, the three together, with no decisions to be made and no loss to be contemplated. He caught himself in the vagrant wish that it could always be so.

But it could not.

Ahead was the lowering, malevolent pit of the great crater. It might as well have been the pits of Hell.

In some dim way—perhaps through his earlier experience with Gailbraith's Oneness—Kirk could sense the Totality, waiting for him.

This was only the advance post of a mental entity which stretched through space to Zaran, and spanned millions of minds. He could sense now a kind of pyramid, held together by psionic science and the bonded females of Sola's kind. It was a pyramid which needed her at its apex—and control of her bond-mate to control her. But if she would not bond with him—or could not, given the counterforce of Spock—then perhaps the Totality could be made to settle for a Starship Captain, which it also wanted.

"I'll go in," Kirk said as they came to the foot of the crater. One side of it had been sheared away into a vertical cliff-face where an engineering masterwork had been performed to tap the massive geo-thermal energies of the live volcano. Without serious effort, the Totality could now mobilize much more than the power of a starship. There would be no way to penetrate this citadel by force. "They want me," Kirk continued. "They've obviously gone to some trouble to get me. They won't harm me. I'll talk. There are enough people in the galaxy who would willingly try a Oneness to make conquest unnecessary."

He stopped, seeing the massive resistance of the other two.

"If anyone goes alone," Spock said, "it must be I, Captain. *You* demonstrably have no defense against Oneness. And you are a primary objective of both Gailbraith's and Soljenov's Ones. They offer no guarantee against harm, and logic suggests that 'talk' is likely to prove less than effectual as a weapon. Your problem would not be to get *in,* but to get *out. Ours* is not to give you as a hostage to fortune. Do you suppose that either of us would not have to come in after you?"

Kirk sighed. *"That* is what has stopped me up to now. But it won't do. The *Enterprise* is at stake, and with it the galaxy. The ship can be used to wipe out the incorrigibles who resist the Totality on Zaran. Millions of lives. And from there it can threaten other planets, other ships. It can become the advance base for taking over other starships. It can be used in our names, using our crew, to discredit the Federation. Wars can be provoked and the Totality can pick up the pieces. Within our lifetimes the Totality can spread through the known galaxy like a cancer. Possibly the Totality could succeed even without Sola, if it had the *Enterprise.* In the face of that, we have to set aside the personal. I am best able to go, and I am in command. You will both remain here."

He turned to go, but Sola's hand settled on his shoulder, and when he turned to look, her eyes locked with his. "No," she said.

"Just—*no?"* Kirk asked, surprised.

"That's right."

"You and what army?" he asked, and if there was the trace of a smile on his lips, he was not amused.

She did not, quite, look at Spock. "You will recall, Captain Kirk," she said, "that your ship and its personnel were placed at my disposal."

It stopped him. "We agreed to attempt not to reach the point which would make you use that authority."

She nodded. "We failed."

"I *have no* ship," he said soberly. "We must assume that the *Enterprise* is under enemy control. Short of a miracle, which we had better perform, all of us will almost certainly fall under alien control. We are three individuals, marooned here, possibly forever, and the rules which applied to a Free Agent and a Starship Captain can't have any real force here. I have my reasons for going in. You will respect that."

"No." She turned to Spock. "Hear me. This is *my* mission and *my* duty. I know how to do it. I cannot do it if impeded by hostages I cannot lose—and who are determined to place themselves in the hands of the enemy. Now that we have all reached this place, Spock, the service you can do for me is to take him, and yourself, to a place of safety, and see me go in."

Spock started to shake his head, but she interrupted him. "Logic, Spock," she said. "I am the galaxy's expert on fighting the Totality. You must let me perform my function. If I were a male, or of a quite incompatible species, you would not stop me. You cannot make what we are to each other the source of the destruction of what we *are*."

The Vulcan looked at her, then at Kirk, and some thought transformed his features. "No. But possibly what we are to each other is our only weapon."

It was their turn to stare at the Vulcan.

"The Totality counted on making her choose," Spock continued. "If she would not, or could not, they must devise a new plan. In an improvised plan, there will always be some flaw. We must go in together."

After a long moment Sola turned to Kirk. "Spock is right. It is my place to go to face the trial. But you—both—are the essence of the trial. I cannot exclude you, nor leave you."

Kirk nodded, but he kept his own counsel about what he would do inside. Spock might be quite right that their threeness was their best weapon.

Or—it might be their most serious danger.

More than likely it was *both* . . .

They turned and looked for a way into the Crater of Hell.

Chapter 28

Soljenov tuned the essence-finder. It brought in the holo-auras of the three target essences, then tuned the bright colors down to a barely perceptible psionic background, and focused on a three-dimensional visual image of the three.

But the Kirlian aura analysis—he still preferred the old Earth term for it—had shown that the female's aura was supercharged with conflict and with insupportable physiological overload. If she were not forced to choose soon, she might well be burned out or destroyed.

Soljenov pressed a button to open a portal in the cliff-face.

The three turned to it. " 'Won't you come into my parlor?' " Kirk quoted. "Let's go."

* * *

Kirk hung back as they came to a fork in the corridor. "Check that branch," he ordered, and Spock and Sola moved in ahead of him.

At the last second he took the other fork, moved down it swiftly and silently, passing a couple of side corridors, then taking one. He found a space behind some installation of machinery where he could conceal himself.

In a moment he heard them looking for him. Heard? He could virtually sense directly their consternation and an undertone of anger. He didn't blame them. It was true that the three had their best strength together. But neither of the other two would permit him to do what he had to do.

He held his breath, but he was almost certain that the mate-hunt sense by which Sola had tracked him was disrupted by Spock's presence. And whatever sense Spock had used to track them both must have led to Sola, and must be further distracted by her. Or so Kirk hoped.

They passed him by and stopped within earshot. For one of the rare times he heard a Vulcan oath-word, and he saw that the Zaran agreed entirely.

"Random search is useless," Sola said. "I have lost the mate-trace and cannot recapture it in your presence or vicinity."

"We must separate."

She made a small sound, not quite a laugh. "There is not sufficient distance, Mr. Spock. Perhaps not in the galaxy."

For a moment they looked at each other.

Then she said, "There is only one place he can ultimately go: to Soljenov. And we must find him there. But first I must do what I thought I would have to go to Zaran to do. Since Soljenov has made this the battlefield, I will do it here. Come."

"What is that?" Spock asked.

She looked up at him. "Earth has a story, of a strong man shorn of his strength by a trick, who regained it to pull a temple down on the heads of his enemies—and himself. If I am right, Spock, I am about to repeat the Samson maneuver —while attempting to avoid the same fate."

She turned and Spock followed her down the hall.

It took whatever Kirk had not to go after them. Whatever stunt she was about to pull was guaranteed to be dangerous to the point of foolhardiness. She was taking on a mental force which included millions of minds—and a physical force which could annihilate her in a moment. Spock might be of some assistance, against both, but even the Vulcan was not an army. And she could not be counted on not to ditch Spock at some point for his protection and go it alone.

She was going up against the impossible—

Kirk bit down on the impulse to go after them and turned the other way. It did not occur to him that the same could be said of him. . . .

McCoy arrived with Dobius and Gailbraith at the foot of the sheer face of the immense crater. The geo-thermal units looked like some immense sculpture in iridium, a gleaming metal god-child construction carelessly attached to the carved crater-face.

McCoy saw the face of Mr. Dobius. "If they can do *this*," the Tanian said, "maybe they have something."

McCoy nodded. "They had, among other things, *you*, Mr. Dobius, or half of you, anyway. And they have, by now, very likely your Captain and First Officer. Can you find a way in?"

Dobius winced. "I shall endeavor, Doctor." He appeared to consult some dim inner sense. His face altered to a pattern of strain McCoy had seen in him once or twice since the takeover. He shifted his phaser within reach of his right hand, and McCoy knew that his left brain was dominant. It was the half which had shown the Totality pattern.

McCoy dropped back beside Gailbraith. "Can you take control back when we need it?"

Gailbraith shrugged. "It remains to be seen. We are at the focal point of an immense Totality—at the point of a cone of mental force having its base on Zaran—tens of millions of minds. My Oneness is a small core of present minds and a tenuous scattering of chosen minds stretching back to the heart-worlds of the Federation. It is my hypothesis that a Choice-Oneness is stronger than a Oneness based partly on force. But that may merely be a hypothesis about the nature of virtue. Such hypotheses may have no basis in fact."

"You mean," McCoy said, "the universe is not necessarily on the side of the good guys?"

"Precisely, Doctor. Worse, the universe, and even the participants, sometimes have some difficulty determining who are the forces of good—or at least who are the future. Virtue has triumphed—on occasion. So, for a time at least, has evil. And sometimes it is difficult to determine whether the new is wrong—or merely different."

McCoy grunted. "I'll grant you that for *your* newness, Ambassador. As far as I know, up to the beginning of this fight you hadn't recruited anybody by force. And I suppose you've been resisting the Totality since. But I won't grant mere 'difference' to the Totality. Force is force."

"What force do you suppose welded together the first successful multicelled animal, Doctor? What if the Totality, right or wrong, is the only catalyst which can bring Oneness to the galaxy?"

"Then it had better not be brought," McCoy said. "It used to be 'my country, right or wrong,' then 'my planet,' 'my empire'—whatever. 'My Totality' doesn't make it any more right—or any less wrong."

Gailbraith turned to him for a moment and bowed fractionally. "My compliments, Doctor. I see now why you are the Captain's friend as well as his ship's surgeon."

McCoy grimaced. "Gailbraith, you'd better get him—all of them—back for me, or you haven't seen anything yet."

They followed Dobius around an outcrop of machinery and came to an open door in the cliff-face.

"Looks like an engraved invitation," McCoy said.

Gailbraith looked interested. "The question is, Doctor: to what?"

"Or—to whom?" McCoy asked. He crouched down to the ground. In the fine volcanic ash which settled under their feet were three sets of footprints—one in soft boots, one of long and narrow feet in Starfleet boots, one in tattered slippers.

McCoy straightened. "To all of us, apparently." He stepped firmly through the door . . .

Soljenov watched the progress of the three with some satisfaction. They were essentially on schedule.

The involvement of the Vulcan with the woman on the level which had been observed had not been predicted. But once seen, it had the quality of the inevitable.

One therefore adjusted the stress test to the metal to be tested—or to the mettle . . .

Kirk moved through the corridors until he saw what he

thought would be a monitor pickup. "Soljenov," he said to it, "I have something you want. I'll deal with you one-on-one."

It took only a moment for Soljenov to answer—confirming Kirk's hypothesis that he would have been watching them from the beginning. "That is rather more like one-on-Oneness, Captain. Scarcely an equal contest."

"I'll risk it. Let them go."

Soljenov laughed. "That would be what the final price might pay for—not an opening subject for negotiation. My parlor is available, Captain. Come in."

Soljenov touched a transporter button and the Captain of the *Enterprise* dissolved to re-form before him, facing him in jungle-tattered rags.

It was given to few men to look impressive in such circumstances. It was given to this one.

"So," Soljenov said, "you are her chosen."

"No. No choice has been made."

"It would have been but for accident of interruption." Soljenov saw the knowledge sink in of what power of observation that must imply. But the Captain merely set his jaw.

"If you know that much, then you know that it was not an unforced choice but a matter of life or death. I do not know that it would have led to bonding, even so. We have our reasons for resistance. We do not take easily to being pawns in your game."

Soljenov laughed. "No. Indeed. Two knights—and one queen. Your pointed-eared 'reason' is rather interesting, by the way."

The man merely looked at him impatiently. "You have my ship. I want her back. And my friend. And Sola—free."

"So—you have come to me alone. To make an offer?"

"At least to talk sense. You cannot have left Earth when you did without learning the horror of forced conquest. Yet you turned to impose it on Zaran, and now on the galaxy. Why?"

"I do not explain my reasons to an amoeba."

Kirk shook his head. "You intend to explain something to this one, or you would not have brought me here."

"Why, no, Captain. I merely intend to take you. Your offer is gallant, but unnecessary. I have the power."

Once again the man merely looked at him with that

impressive courage. "That may be," he said, "and I knew that coming in. But I do not think that I would be easy to absorb—or digest. I submit that you do need some terms with me."

Soljenov shrugged. "No. But for a purpose of my own, I will answer your question. I once rebelled against the force I saw used in the old empires of Earth. For that rebellion it became necessary for us to flee Earth. Myself, a friend, a small party. After the long sleep we came to Zaran, and it welcomed us. We brought a physical technology, Zaran already had a high psycho-psionic and ecologic technology. For a time a perfect marriage. Then we discovered the possibility of true Oneness, Totality, belonging. Ultimately, that is the only answer to the horrors we have seen engulfing entire populations—conquest, war, concentration camps, genocide."

Kirk looked at him without belief. "You argue the conquest of the Totality as an *answer* to conquest?"

"Captain, I assure you, it is the only answer. There is an occasional brief mental resistance before some of the more stubborn join the Totality. Once joined, most accept its pleasures and powers. It is a long-term answer to loneliness, isolation, powerlessness, and to sickness, old age—even death."

"At the price of individuality, greatness, genius, passion, love."

Soljenov smiled. "Does it destroy passion, Captain—or even love? You will not know until you are One. Has it not occurred to you that *that* would be the solution to your particular immediate problem? In Totality, Captain, none of you would have to sacrifice or lose."

Kirk did not answer. Then he said, "Very well. Even that has occurred to me. But it would not and will not work. Sola and Spock are to go free. So is my ship."

"You see, Captain, that thought will occur, even to you. Eventually it will occur to the galaxy. You tasted Gailbraith's Oneness—and only your Vulcan friend was able to pull you back. Do you doubt, then, the power of Oneness? Or that the Totality will, shortly, sweep the galaxy? Bringing, finally, peace? That, Captain, is worth a little initial discomfort for amoebas—or tarnish of soul, if that is what it is, for me."

"Then you do believe it tarnishes your soul."

"If so, I will bear it."

"No," Kirk said. "That kind of peace, even if it could exist, would not be worth it. And that argument—that you have to break eggs to make an omelette, or amoebas to make a Oneness—has been the argument of every dictator, every totalitarian from Hitler and Stalin to the ones you fought, to Colonel Green and all the others. But intelligent beings are not eggs—nor amoebas—and when they break, the irreplaceable is lost, and the unforgivable is done. Soljenov, don't you see that you have bought the argument of your old enemies?"

"They had no reality of Oneness. *I* have."

"Yes. And it *is*, for some people, as powerful and as attractive as you say. Perhaps it is for almost anyone at the right time, in the right way. Yes, I felt the attraction. But those who will join you willingly, you may have. No one contests that. Let Gailbraith's Oneness exist, and yours, and uncounted others—and add to the welcome diversity of the galaxy. But let the unwilling go."

Soljenov shook his head. "You do not understand, Captain. That was my first thought, also. But the singletons find Oneness an intolerable threat, and will turn to destroy it in its infancy, if permitted. And a plurality of Onenesses may turn out to be even more dangerous than a plurality of singletons. Do you suppose that my will and Gailbraith's would never lock at cross-purposes? It has begun to do so already. Over you and your ship. What about over a galaxy? No. There must be one answer—and one Oneness. The Totality. All else is chaos. Captain, I have had enough of chaos."

"You will have no end of chaos until you abandon force."

Soljenov cut him short. "I am not here to be instructed by an amoeba. State your offer."

"My ship, Sola, Spock, Gailbraith's Oneness, and the Zaran resistance to go free. I will come into the Totality—and you and I will have this out—for as long as it takes."

Soljenov laughed. "Everything? For your single person? You do not underestimate yourself, Captain."

Kirk shrugged. "You have set this up, through Gailbraith, to bring me here. I do not fully know why. Perhaps I am your antithesis, your test case, your symbol. In any case, you have set a value on me, and I have made an offer on the only terms that are possible for me."

"I will consider it, Captain. Later."

"Later it may not be open."

"Later I may have all three of you."

"Gailbraith said you were setting up a trial," Kirk said. "Why? A trial implies that you have something to learn."

"That is perceptive, Captain. I do. My belief in the necessity of Oneness does not compel the universe to agree. My purpose requires Sola. She is the climax of the line of Zaran females which can widen the scope of total unity far beyond Zaran. If I prove that it is possible, it is a means which the chosen Onenesses have not found. Gailbraith's kind remains limited in scope. If I have abolished the limits, he will concede the validity of the method and join me. Then nothing can stop Totality."

"Sola will not join you."

Soljenov smiled. "You mistake the point, Captain. It was always possible to control Sola, if she would bond. However, she was, at various times, offered all that Zaran, or even certain other species, could offer, to no avail."

Kirk frowned. "All Zaran could offer? Did that include *you?*"

Soljenov was silent for a moment. "Yes, Captain, it did."

"Did you—love her?"

"Captain, I will not discuss that with you. Let us say that I needed her—for my purpose."

"And she could not be moved."

There was another moment's silence. "She could be, eventually, Captain. I searched the galaxy for the lever, and found not one, but two."

"Mr. Spock is not a tool for your use, Soljenov. And he is a refutation of your theory. You did not expect him—not that Sola would love him, nor he her. If your theory is wrong, you must let them go."

"On the contrary, Captain. I think it likely that the pull of the duality will unleash Sola's powers as no single love could. And perhaps when it becomes impossible for her . . ." Soljenov turned away. "It is rather hard on you and your Vulcan friend, Captain. I express regret, but I cannot spare you. The next phase of the trial is about to begin."

"That's right," Kirk said softly, and moved to bring a chopping hand down on Soljenov's shoulder.

It was as if the edge of his hand had impacted on the entire Totality.

Soljenov merely turned to look at him. Then for one moment Kirk saw something in the big man's eyes which he knew was lethal: the knowledge that Soljenov had taken some turning by which he, with all his power, could not evoke in Sola what one particular amoeba *could* evoke. In fact, what *two* particular amoebas could call forth, including a Vulcan who was not supposed to know the meaning of love.

Then Soljenov's hands clamped down on Kirk with a grip which also seemed to have the power of all of the Totality, or perhaps only of the man's own strength . . .

Chapter 29

At a psi-marked junction in a corridor Sola stopped Spock.
"This is as far as you can go."

"Indeed?" the Vulcan said, and she saw the stubbornness
of all Vulcan settle into his face. "On what do you base that
conclusion?"

"This is a Focal Center of the Totality," she said. "Beyond
this point there is no functioning as a semi-independent unit.
Here the powers of Zaran females are focused on some
physical-psionic device to give total control over all who
enter. By mind-to-mind contact the smallest intention to act
outside the demands of Totality is known and is met by instant
punishment. Obedience is rewarded. Reward and punishment are transmitted directly to the brain's pain and pleasure

centers, psionically. It is as if an electrical signal stimulated direct pain and direct pleasure."

Spock's mouth was tight. "That has been done by direct electrical stimulation—long before Soljenov left Earth, in the twentieth century. Rats would press a lever for direct pleasure, ignoring food, sleep, sex, until they starved to death."

Sola nodded. "No one has broken the control of a Focal Center. They are used wherever total security or total obedience is required. On ships. In critical installations. In battle. Men will march into the jaws of death rather than face direct pain. And direct pleasure is, if anything, more insidious.

"Mr. Spock, picture the *Enterprise* controlled by an obscenity of this kind. Picture its Captain, also controlled. *You* might conceivably die before being absorbed. *He* would not. And perhaps you would not, either, knowing whom you would leave to what fate." She leveled her shoulders. "This must stop here, Spock, and *I* must stop it. If I can break the psionic control, then some of those who see me do it may be able to do the same. Zaran females may break free. Some Zaran may put his hand with mine to smash this place."

"*May*," Spock said. "Until that point, every man's hand will be against you—and every mind of the Totality."

She nodded. "Spock, it is a method of control developed and tested on rats. There is a flaw in that theory."

He raised an inquiring eyebrow.

"A man," she said, "is not a rat. Nor am I."

For a moment his eyes approved her. "Agreed. Very well. We go together."

She shook her head. "Even the disciplines of Vulcan are no protection here. As a male you are more vulnerable. As a male to whom I am drawn, you would make it impossible for me. They would use that against me in the first instant. The one thing you can do for me is to remain out here, as my life-line, so that I will know I *must* make it back out here to you. Nothing else would bring me out."

"*No one* else?" Spock asked.

She met his eyes. "Him. But they may use him against me in any case. In that event, you will be the only anchor—for both of us."

He was silent for a very long space of heartbeats. She saw whole empires of Vulcan theory rise and fall behind his eyes, and then he rebuilt in an architecture which was purely his own. "If I were not a Vulcan," he said, "perhaps I would know how to tell you how much I need to be a Vulcan, now."

She laughed silently. "Another non-Vulcan thing you've managed very well, Mr. Spock." She reached up and for one moment brushed her lips against his. "If I do not return in thirty minutes, Spock, find him and get out of the mountain. Do not look or wait for me. The inner chambers of the tree-caves may survive."

"We will not go without you."

Her eyes went hard. "You *will*, or you will reckon with me. I will have my own means."

"Shall I live—knowing that you lied?"

Yes, Mr. Spock, she said. But aloud she lied without reservation, even on the unspoken levels between them. "If I am not back, I will have failed, and I will be in no great danger. The Totality has use for me. Go."

Then she turned and went, not giving him further chance to protest, or to detect a lie.

Spock watched her move down the corridor, head high, and only the knowledge of the use they would make of him against her held him.

Even of that he was not certain. There were the disciplines of Vulcan. He reached deep within himself in the manner of everything which he had been taught or had ever learned, summoning the strength of Vulcan against everything here which conspired to erode it. *I am Vulcan. I control.*

He saw Sola shudder, as if buffeted by invisible forces. He moved forward until he felt the psionic field, like a palpable entity. He could touch it with his hands. He put his hands against it, into it, and let his mind reach out, cautiously.

Entity, one entity. Yes. Millions in One. Now the One was aware of the tiny female one who came to challenge, and of the alien who reached out and sought to send her his strength.

In a sudden wrench of perspective, Spock looked out from Sola's eyes, aware both of himself and of her inner battle. She moved by an effort of will. Tendrils of the Oneness reached out insidiously to penetrate her mind, to reach down into the nerve centers of her brain. No armoring would stand against them, and she had known that. Resistance delayed the full effect, but would not stop it.

Spock sensed, abruptly, that the tendrils which reached for the direct pain centers were as she had described, but even more appalling than he had contemplated.

But it was the tendrils which reached for the pleasure centers which were far more insidious even than he had conceived. They searched now for every exquisite center of being, every sensation, every enjoyment, every delight ever known or desired or beyond daring to desire. Then he saw that it was not even merely the physical which they reached for. Somewhere deep within was that most guarded center by which the Zaran female would bond in a Oneness beyond other species, and by which Sola, with her inheritance and her outworld training, would bond in a way known to no other Zaran female.

Spock could sense that bonding center now, open and vulnerable, and stretched taut by a pull of two longings, for which it had never been designed. That divided heart was her weakness now, the weakness for which she had never trained, which she could never have expected. She had armored herself against every ordinary temptation, and her particular devil had found the one man, one temptation, against which she was not proof—and then by luck or oversight had found also the Vulcan who had never expected to be her second temptation.

Spock moved instinctively to offer some protection for that vulnerability, throwing his own resistance against the tendril which reached down into her mind to search it out.

The tendril paused—and then the great Oneness behind it sensed the Vulcan mind and split off an electrifying tendril to search it out. Suddenly, Spock sensed it reaching far down into his own mind, toward the Vulcan center which was also a bonding center, also open and vulnerable now.

In a moment the electric connection would be made between them—under the control of the Totality.

Spock flung himself bodily back out of the field. It was all he could do. He felt the connection snap at the last instant with a wrench which crumpled him to the floor and left him alone in his own body.

He saw Sola, far down the corridor, sag to her knees. Then after a very long space, she lifted her head. She turned to look back at him, and he saw no reproach in her eyes, as if she knew he had had to test it. Now they both knew: he could not be with her in this.

She made it to her feet and disappeared around the corner.

Spock stood up more slowly. The wrench of contradiction was still pulling at him. He was forbidden to feel what he did, in fact, feel. And this time it could not be covered or denied or merely lived with, as he had done with other forbidden feelings, all those years.

Nor could this feeling be permitted.

He performed the discipline of control again, for all the good it did him. And this time he set himself to look for Kirk. Spock could not be with Sola, but he had tasted the power of what she went against. If it were used against Kirk, or if Kirk were used against *her*—there would be no hope, unless Spock could find him.

Spock moved off down the corridor, setting himself into that state in which he moved almost beyond the direction of his own will, following some instinct by which he had once or twice been able to find what he needed to find.

The search assumed that Kirk had not already been absorbed by—or given himself to—the Totality.

It was an assumption not in evidence, Spock warned himself sternly. He knew only too well what bargain Kirk would have tried to make, for his ship and for the two lives he thought he would set free.

Spock permitted himself to hope that the Human could feel the force of Vulcan anger from here. . . .

Chapter 30

Sola confronted the young Watcher at the door. "Take me to your Center," she said.

The young man was golden and fair—and he was very young and very earnest. He roused from some inner control by the Totality to look at her for a moment with his own eyes. They were grave, blue-gray eyes which, in other circumstances, would have taken responsibility for his actions, and he attempted to do so even here.

"I do not anticipate you here," he said. "What is your errand?"

She smiled into the grave young eyes. "I will tell you, presently. What is your name?"

The youngster looked as if he had forgotten how to hear that question. But her asking it reminded him of a time and life in which his name had been important. And he knew that her asking made it important again. The question acknowledged what she saw in him not as unit but as one special entity, one man.

"Argunov," he said.

Some warning clouded behind his eyes as if the Totality sensed that this unit was about to malfunction. He shook it off and looked into her eyes directly. "What is your name?" he managed.

"Sola Thane," she said, and saw his eyes light for an instant.

"Here?" he said.

Then the pain struck him, driving him to the floor. It reached for her, too, but the searing tendrils were not fully set yet, and she was able to set her teeth and kneel down to hold his shoulders.

After a time the worst of it left him, and he looked up into her eyes. "You moved against the pain," he said, astonished. "And—you held me."

She stood up and gave him her hand, helping him to his feet. "And *you,*" she said, "knew my name, even here. Come, Argunov."

He debated it with himself. "I must know your purpose."

"To prove that what it meant when I asked your name is real."

"I have no power to help you," he said. "But it is considered my function to bring the unexpected to my Central. I will do so."

She let her eyes acknowledge his meaning. "That is all I asked."

He moved with her through the corridors, for that moment recovering the easy, confident stride of his young manhood. He was of Human descent, she saw, born on Zaran to its conquerors, but now himself finding the Totality an uneasy home.

It was for the Argunovs that she had come back from Starfleet and the stars.

Now she felt the solid core of the Totality's Focal Center focusing its resistance on her, until the psionic field was like a thick molasses, slowing their movement. The probing tendrils moved deeper into her mind, and she knew that she would no longer escape the worst which the pain—or pleasure—could do.

Then the corridor opened out into a great lava vault, now honeycombed with machinery and the activity of controlled Workers servicing it.

In the center of it all stood a Zaran woman. She was as tall as Sola, lithe and strong, but her hair was beginning to show the white-gold of age.

Her green-gold eyes looked older than her hair.

In the thick psionic field of the Focal Center, Sola could sense the tie which bound this woman here. Once she had resisted the Humans, then she had loved one—and come to believe in the Totality, in the Oneness. Perhaps she still believed in its goal. What she believed had become irrelevant. She was mate-bonded. Her mate was of the Totality, and he was in its power.

"I bring the unknown," Argunov said to her.

The older Zaran's eyes conceded nothing. "You have troubled yourself to learn the name of the unknown, Watcher," she said.

Argunov met the eyes. "That is true. She has troubled herself to know mine."

"That is not merely trouble, Watcher," the Zaran Center said. "It is a breach of One-spirit. Your service does not require the distinction of a name." She turned to Sola. "*Your* name is known to me, and it is the name of a traitor. You have brought other-worlders here, and your intent is to destroy the Totality which serves your people."

"My intent, Z'Ehlah," Sola said, "is to free my people. If that be treason, you are welcome to make the most of it. I have come here to the Center of your power. Treason cannot live here. But I *can.*"

"So you also know my name, So'lathane. Then you know that I will oppose you. You can live here only as One."

"I know that you defend your mate, Z'Ehlah. But you do it at the cost of the Argunovs, and now of the galaxy. You will take no more ships. And you will release the *Enterprise.* I also know defense of mate."

"Of *which* mate?" Z'Ehlah asked. "You attempt to walk in two directions. It is the formula for a fall."

"Then I will fall," Sola said. "But I will take all of this

down with me." She gestured to the whole installation. Then she turned to Argunov. "Argunov, you knew my name before I came. You chafe at Totality. Why have you never moved against it?"

Argunov stood straight. "I have believed, or tried to believe, that the Oneness was right, or was at least necessary. And in any moment when I could not believe it—I knew there was no possibility of resistance."

She turned back to Z'Ehlah. "I will not ask *you* why. I know why. I will not ask you to stand aside. But I must go through you."

Beyond Z'Ehlah was the control panel for the geo-thermal units. "Then that is what you will have to do," the Zaran woman said.

Z'Ehlah set herself, physically and psionically. Sola could feel the force flowing through the Zaran woman, and now she could see the thin gold band of electrodes which was almost hidden by the other woman's white-gold mane. It must focus broadcast power to amplify the Zaran's bonding capacity to bring the hunting band together. Now it hunted ships—and souls. And it hunted the soul of So'lathane of Zaran.

Sola felt Z'Ehlah reach out and gather up the force of countless minds, then direct it at her in one blow of crushing force.

Sola stood under it, not as if it did not touch her, but as if it could not matter that it did. She had known it would come, the full trial against direct pain, and now it was here. . . .

Kirk sank to his knees as if poleaxed, his body suddenly a mass of pain. It was all he could do not to scream. He was not certain that he would not—nor that he had not.

Soljenov bent down and pulled him roughly to his feet. "Do you still wish to mate-bond with a Zaran?"

Kirk did not answer. He knew now that it was Sola's pain he felt. She was dying— No, it was worse than that, for this mortal agony could be prolonged forever, and never broken. "Let her go!" he whispered harshly.

Soljenov smiled bitterly. "She challenges the Totality. We are expected to see the error of our ways and desist. Not so, Captain. You will presently participate in a small experiment in incorruptibility of soul. If any."

He caught Kirk's arm and propelled him through the corridors toward the interior of the crater.

Spock sagged against the wall. The pain was an overload even for his Vulcan capacity to control. He tried to send his control to her, but he knew that nothing could reach her. This was her fight, alone.

And somewhere ahead, clearly now, as if by a three-way circuit, he sensed Kirk, also caught in the transference of Sola's trial by fire.

Spock moved ahead while he had the direction.

Argunov stepped forward and held Sola as she sagged. He caught her against his body and held her as if he could absorb her pain into his own body.

He could not, and the Center did not even divert force to send him his own punishment. It would come. He saw other Watchers, Workers, Joiners, turn to look at him as if he had taken leave of his senses—and at *her* as if she had never had any.

They sensed in the thick psionic field the titanic effort to take over So'lathane's mind. Z'Ehlah would not yield, could not.

Yet neither could Sola.

Close as he was, Argunov sensed even the fine threads of contact which stretched to the two off-world men. For a moment he felt the stab of a fierce possessiveness, as if he would hold her even against that pull.

But it was those threads which anchored her.

'Yield,' Z'Ehlah demanded silently.

No one spoke by voice or mind-speech under the punishment. One yielded by yielding. There was no alternative.

Argunov felt Sola's head lift slowly from his shoulder.

'No,' she said.

Argunov sensed Z'Ehlah's shock. Resistance was not possible. And the force of the punishment was already at a level beyond increase. In a matter of seconds it would build to the point of irreversible shock and death . . .

"Let her go," Kirk grated. "Take *me*."

From somewhere he sensed a 'No!' in a mind-voice he

knew. Spock! Then he was alive, near. Kirk tried to warn him off.

'Soljenov!' the silent voice projected. 'A Vulcan to serve you would challenge you. Let them both go.'

Soljenov laughed. "Such nobility."

"She's *dying*," Kirk whispered. He himself was held up only by some stubborness—and Soljenov's hand.

Soljenov shrugged. "That is not my plan."

Kirk sensed an order go out—and suddenly his pain stopped, so abruptly that he sagged with relief.

Chapter 31

Sola straightened in the young man's arms. Argunov had held her, and now she felt punishment about to fall on him.

"No," she said, almost without voice. "Whatever you do is to be done to *me*, alone."

"It is *not*," Z'Ehlah said. "Your two are with you."

Sola lifted her head. "I know it. Let the trial stop with me."

Z'Ehlah shook her head. "That is not my choice, it is yours. And you have made it."

"No," Sola said, "I have not chosen."

Z'Ehlah looked at her almost with astonishment. "Is it possible you do not know? You are attempting to choose *both*."

"That is biologically impossible," Sola said. "I am Zaran."

"It is impossible, and it may take all three of you to destruction, but that is your attempt."

Sola focused on being able to stand away from Argunov and move.

"Thank you," she said to him, and for a moment focused on his face, perhaps as a reminder of other faces. Here was one which might have commanded a starship, one day, and never would, unless she could show him how to free himself now. She moved toward Z'Ehlah.

Z'Ehlah moved back slightly, not yielding, merely giving ground. "You must know," she said, "that the direct pain is merely pain. Rebels have defied pain, even to the death, before. It is the pleasure which is unendurable, and unbeatable. It will make you want it beyond any other pleasure. You cannot get past it."

Sola lifted her head. "I can. *I*—have known the real thing." She knew then that only the events of this day would let her say that, and that those memories alone would get her through this.

For a moment Sola saw something in Z'Ehlah's eyes which might have been regret, remembrance. Was there a time when the reality of her mate had been beyond anything which the Totality could offer?

Sola took a step forward and the Zaran Center gathered all the forces of the Focal Point for the last defense.

Then the power burned through her mind in one searing sheet of flame, an ecstasy so intense that it resembled pain. Tendrils reached down deep, even into the bonding center. And against the false pleasure she could summon only the reality. *Spock!* she said to herself, and then for the first time permitted herself the name, *Jim!*

But she seemed to have lost the thread of mental contact. She could summon only the memories. And even those seemed to fade against the overwhelming neurological assault of direct pleasure. She had only to allow it, and that peak state which an intelligent being is fortunate to reach for moments out of a lifetime could be hers whenever she summoned or earned it. She could understand the rat who kept pressing the pleasure lever.

She felt her body shake as with some dreadful neurological disease, a palsied, paralyzed state which could only stand—stopped and defeated.

She felt Argunov hold her shoulders, sensed his young despair. For a moment he had believed in her.

She summoned his face before her blinded eyes, and then another face, Vulcan—Vulcan eyes, Vulcan arms . . .

Sola opened her eyes and took a step forward. She moved like a stroke victim learning how to walk, moving over and beyond the messages scrambled by a ravaged brain. But she moved.

Jim! Human eyes. Human lips, and the taste of his fight with fire-dragons and his own demons of jealousy—and sacrifice.

She moved.

Now she saw Z'Ehlah, all but paralyzed with the effort to stop her, and by an almost metaphysical dread which said that Sola could not do this. For if she could, then Z'Ehlah could perhaps have broken the control, long ago. Her mate could have been free—

Sola moved past the shaken Z'Ehlah suddenly, in one lunge, and reached the control panel. She slashed her hand down across switches to cut out safety overrides, then shorted out the panel.

She heard a Zaran transporter hum behind her.

She was just touching the large purple lever which was the main power overload, when a hand fell on her and flung her away from the panel.

It was Soljenov.

"You were faster than I thought, my dear," he said tightly. He started to reach for the panel to undo the worst damage. Young Argunov dived past him and pulled down the purple lever.

Flames shot up, and something rumbled suddenly, ominously, within the crater. Half the lights flared high and then blacked out. The floor shook.

Soljenov turned on the young Watcher in astonishment. Then he himself focused a burn-out intensity of the direct pleasure on Argunov. The youngster stiffened and started to crumple, but Sola was suddenly there, catching his shoulders and looking into his eyes.

"Argunov!" she said. "Come. Break it."

Slowly the blue-gray eyes focused on her. Argunov fought to move and the palsy caught him. He shook under her hands. Then his eyes flamed up in one savage blast of fury at a long captivity which he knew suddenly held him only by his compliance.

He took a step forward, almost into her arms, and she held him for one instant and then turned with him to face Soljenov.

She could feel the shock spreading in ripples through the Totality Focal Center. For the first time the units had seen someone defy the unity. There was a young Zaran woman bent over a communications panel nearby. Suddenly she stood up and moved toward Argunov and Sola.

Z'Ehlah rallied to turn the pleasure signal on the young communications technician. She looked straight at Sola as the shaking nearly pulled her down—but she kept moving.

Sola turned back to Soljenov. But he did not look as worried as he should have. Indeed, he looked as if he held his quarry in his hand.

Suddenly the ground shifted and a crack opened in the floor. It belched sudden heat and an ominous steam.

Soljenov looked almost pleased. "I am finished with this installation, my dear—and with all who do not stand with me. I am taking the starship. You have now set yourself a time-limit for solving a certain problem."

He stepped to the communications panel and threw switches.

The holo-spaces above the console filled with life-size figures. Then backed up to show that each of them was stranded on two separate ledges divided by a chasm too wide to jump—and by a slowly rising flow of lava which eroded their ledges.

The Human figure was only partly conscious. But the Vulcan was fully conscious—of his own helplessness. He could not reach the Human. And if he had wanted to escape alone, his way back out was blocked by the psionic field of the Totality Focal Center. Not even Spock, much less Kirk, could have moved through it unaided.

And in minutes their ledges would collapse into the lava flow—if another quake did not get them first.

"So there it is, my dear," Soljenov said. "You may save one of them, but only one, for it can only be done by bonding with one of them. Bonded, you might bring him through the Focal Field, alive. No other way."

She did not pause to listen. She ran. The Totality Field

could not stop her now, and she had the thread of direction, two threads.

It was not far to go, but it was the longest trip she had made. She dodged through breathless, airless corridors, reeking with steam and sulfur like the pits of the Human's Hell—or of parts of the Vulcan's home planet.

But it was Hell, here. She knew there was no salvation, for any of them. In moments she arrived on a third tongue of ledge, almost directly between them, the lava flow dividing around her ledge, almost at her feet.

Kirk was conscious now, and she was the first thing he saw. "Sola, get out of here!" He was all but naked and looked as if he had been dragged through jungle.

Then he caught the direction of her other look and looked over his shoulder to see Spock. He swore, once, short and sharp.

"Take him out," Spock said. "He can reach you along that ledge when you have bonded with him." Spock pointed out a toehold ledge of collapsed corridor, with a few handholds above, which an extremely active man might have made with no interference and every assistance. It might as well have been sealed off from Kirk by a wall. In fact, it *was*. The moment he moved toward it he would hit the Totality Focal Field.

If he were bonded with her, she might conceivably shield him enough for him to make it. She could not shield both of them. Spock did not point it out, but she saw a slender conduit which sagged out from Spock's ledge to within fifteen feet of her own. If it would hold his weight and he made no false move, there was some possibility that he could tightrope-walk it and jump far enough. But the Focal Field would get him, too, before he had gone two steps.

Kirk saw it, too. "Spock can make it along that conduit. Get him first." He crawled closer to the edge of his ledge—and hit the field. Then he understood. He flung himself back out of it and looked at her. "So—that's it." His eyes narrowed. "What Spock said—does that mean you could get him out by bonding with him?"

She looked at him bleakly. "I could bring one of you out, or try to. Only one. By bonding."

"Then it must be Spock," Kirk said immediately.

"It cannot be," Spock interposed. "We established that,

long ago." To Sola he said, "You must take him and go. While you occupy the attention of the Focal Field, I will be able to move by my own Vulcan powers. Go."

It was a good try, and a refutation in itself of the legend that Vulcans cannot lie. She did not immediately dispute the point. If she chose Kirk, his belief in that lie was the only possible chance that she could get Kirk to move.

"Mr. Spock," Kirk said, "is lying in his Vulcan teeth. It won't work. I won't budge. But if you two will get the hell out in time, *I* may stand a good chance." He turned to the Vulcan. "Mr. Spock, you are to proceed out of here immediately by the means available, without argument. That is an order."

Spock looked at him for what seemed a long time. "I am unable to comply, Captain," he said. "Some things transcend the discipline of the service."

Sola looked from one to the other. It was in her hands now. Her choice—with finality.

She knew then that she could not choose. She would have traded places with either of them, not to have to choose. And if she did not choose, both would die. And she with them, for she would not leave.

Yet there was no way to choose. Stray bits of memory kept coming back to her: her first sight of Kirk in the clearing, his white face and look of keeping on keeping on—and the sudden look of that strain lifting as he learned what, and who, she was . . . Kirk, coming back essentially from death in the scoutship, because she would not let him go . . . Kirk sending her back to unlock the chains and scatter the vultures until Spock was truly free . . . Kirk in the tree-cave of the fire-dragon . . . Kirk jumping down beside them into the midst of the ten-foot manlings, with his puny club—going to fight the leopard. And Kirk—coming here, to offer himself to the Totality, for the freedom and happiness of his friend, with the woman he loved. . . .

But there was Spock. She also had seen him dragging chains, rock, vultures, and all, and she had seen him break free, if only for a moment. In that moment he had been open and vulnerable, and in her hands. And he had not taken refuge behind the great wall of Vulcan and gone quietly off to die in the face of his contradiction. He had faced it, and her, head-on. And he had never for a moment forgotten Kirk or what price Kirk had been willing to pay for Spock's freedom.

It came to her suddenly that there was no way to choose between two such men. Any choice was treason to the value of the other one. Worse, the one she did not choose would know that she had not chosen him. And the one she chose would hate her for the death of the other half of himself.

Yet to refuse to choose was treason to both.

She would have to choose—now. And do it quickly before the one she chose could stop her. . . .

Then a voice spoke in her mind. 'So. You perceive the difficulty of the problem.' It was Soljenov.

'Yes,' she said silently. Then his image formed in a one-way hologram in front of her. Kirk and Spock would not see or hear him.

Soljenov laughed silently. 'This is the true Devil's dilemma, my dear. You had thought Gailbraith was your personal Devil. You were wrong. *I* am. What would you pay never to have them know your choice—because you would not have to make it?'

She felt her throat tighten. 'What are you asking?'

'More than your soul.'

McCoy struggled with a nightmare sense of Oneness. He had gotten what he had bargained for, in spades.

They had reached the point where McCoy and Dobius could no longer proceed. There was some kind of psionic field which did not register on McCoy's scanners, but gave him the personal collywobbles. Whatever that was. In this case, his legs wouldn't track.

Neither would the long legs of Mr. Dobius. They were caught somewhere between right brain and left brain. The big Tanian stalled out and stood numbly.

Gailbraith possibly could have moved into the field, but he stopped for them. "You were to experience Oneness," he said to McCoy. "It is time."

He reached out to touch McCoy's face and McCoy clamped his jaw and didn't fight it. "Get them *out*," he said.

"We must first get *in*—through Mr. Dobius," Gailbraith said.

Then his mind reached out and dissolved McCoy's consciousness into the edges of Oneness. It was terrifying, but not unpleasant. He found he could look through Gailbraith's eyes, sense the big man's body, sense his intentness on a purpose. Then he gathered McCoy up with him and both of them looked out of one of Mr. Dobius' eyes. They must be in his brain-half which was controlled by Gailbraith's Oneness.

Then they shifted across into the other half of the brain, and McCoy knew suddenly that they were within the Totality. He felt the enormous flowing of mental force—and then he sensed sudden eddies, torrents, confusion, even rebellion.

The Totality was in an uproar. And it knew in every individual cell that the volcano was giving way. But the individual cells were held to their posts by Soljenov.

Then abruptly, they were in Soljenov's perspective. He seemed to be hanging in space over a torrent of fire—facing Sola Thane, who was standing on a ledge above molten lava.

Then Soljenov became aware of Gailbraith and company. Soljenov turned around and his holographic perspective turned with him until McCoy could see through his eyes. The two men trapped on separate ledges: Kirk and Spock. Soljenov seemed to speak aloud for their benefit. And McCoy caught the flash of a thought which ordered a hologram of Gailbraith, McCoy, and Dobius to be found through the monitors and projected to face his own. In moments, as he spoke, it was done, and McCoy saw Kirk, Sola, and Spock see himself and Gailbraith in the new hologram. McCoy could still sense dimly the thoughts of Gailbraith and his One, and of Soljenov, but now he also seemed to see with his own eyes.

"You will note, Gailbraith, Doctor, and associate," Soljenov said to them, "that a trial has been set. The only means of saving either man is for Sola to bond with one of them, and in either case, I will then have my bonded-female as weapon—the culmination of the Z line of descent of Zaran females, bonded strongly to a male in a life-or-death choice. With Sola Thane, Ambassador Gailbraith, Oneness comes to the galaxy in both our lifetimes. War ends. All of the concerns of singletons become old and void. The *galaxy* becomes new—the playground of the new multicellular life."

"*If* I also join you," Gailbraith said. "Otherwise it becomes a contest for the survival of the fittest multicellular life. That would push evolution still further, perhaps. Or it would create a struggle of Titans to make all of the singleton struggles of all time look puny and bloodless."

Soljenov smiled grimly. "Precisely. That war of Titans would make Armageddon look like a preliminary event. There is no compromise, Gailbraith. Your fine vision of a plurality of Onenesses will not work. There must be one Total entity. Ultimately it must be galaxywide, or there will be a war of all against all. And only the Totality, with the final power which Sola Thane will bring it, can become that entity."

"Why?" Kirk asked suddenly from his ledge. He had a bone-white look which McCoy didn't like, but Kirk found strength somewhere for that flare of passionate thought which had turned tides for them before. *"Why* should plurality and diversity mean enmity? Even we singletons have learned friendship, love—a oneness which does not have to mean Oneness. For us, at least, Oneness means the end of the unique entity—dehumanizing, depersonalizing loss of identity. But our kind of oneness"—he gestured toward Sola and Spock—"is a celebration of individual identity, of difference. There is no love, no passion, no friendship, no ultimate personal choice which does not depend on the unique, irreplaceable *one.* It is what we would miss in Oneness, and why we have fought against you with our lives. But why shouldn't two diverse Onenesses also begin to find that in each other? What would prevent friendship between the unique entities of Oneness—friendship, perhaps even love?"

"Power prevents," Soljenov said. "An entity grows. Or dies."

"Infants and children grow," Kirk said. "Adults—love."

Soljenov shrugged. "You may have the good fortune to be an adult of your species, Captain. I am an infant of mine. The adult form of my species is not yet known. Does the caterpillar envision the butterfly? Yet the caterpillar must spin its cocoon. And I must spin mine." He looked at Sola. "We digress. You have not much time, and they"—he indicated Kirk and Spock—"have less. Your decision?"

"Sola," Kirk said urgently, "make no bargains. Take Spock. I will be all right."

She turned to him. "What bargain would *you* then make,

and with whom? No. If I refuse Soljenov, he *will* let you die. And do you suppose there would be anything left for the other two of us then?"

"That is right," Spock said. "Get the Captain out. I shall make it under my own power."

"'And shall I live knowing that you lied,' Spock?" Sola said, as if it were a quotation between them.

Spock's eyes went bleak. "If necessary. But *live*. Get him out."

She turned to Soljenov. *"I will not choose between them,"* she said.

"Then you choose the death of both," Soljenov said. "Or you accept my terms."

"I—" Sola began.

"No!" Kirk thundered. "Soljenov, you wanted a soul. All right. You have found my price. I won't promise not to fight you from within. But you will have me where you wanted me. I will become part of the Totality, or of Gailbraith's One—or perhaps the bridge to join both. I suspect that might influence Gailbraith to join you. My ship, Sola, and Spock are to go free—whether they like it or not."

Soljenov smiled. "Interesting, Captain. Do you believe that your soul is so valuable to me?"

"Yes," Kirk said.

"Gailbraith," Soljenov asked, "is it true that you would welcome the Captain as a bridge between us?"

"Possibly," Gailbraith said, "if he becomes part of my Oneness first."

"And if you then fail to join me?" Soljenov asked.

"I am weighing a question," Gailbraith said. "When it is answered, I will tell you what it was—and name my decision."

Soljenov laughed. "When I have answered a question of my own, and *if* I accept the Captain's as the best offer—I might let you have him."

Spock turned to Kirk across the gulf and the Vulcan's eyes were hard. "I do not require or accept sacrifice."

Kirk met his eyes across the gulf. "I do not *make* one. I have—acquired a taste for oneness. Or Oneness. It is an elegant solution to an otherwise insoluble problem, Spock. The three of us have struggled with that problem, to no solution. There is no solution within our normal parameters. I cannot take her from you—or see her with you. I can't leave. You can't. She can't. Impasse. But nothing is won without cost. I will free the ship and settle with the question of Oneness. I do not think the Totality can continue its present course if I am in it. And this way—I will not be alone. Nor will you.''

Spock stepped to the edge of his ledge. "At the first attempt to implement such a decision, Jim," he said levelly, "I will make it a null solution." He looked down into the flowing lava below.

"Spock!" Kirk yelled.

"That option is closed," Sola said quickly, stepping to the edge of her own ledge. "Soljenov, neither one of them can be yours." She lifted her head, and McCoy knew that he would remember that look forever. "Nor—*mine*," she said.

"Sola—" Spock said. It was the first time McCoy remembered hearing Spock speak that name. He wondered if it would be the last . . . ?

"They both have their mission and life-path," Sola said. "And I have mine. Our paths have intersected—and now must diverge again. I could not stay—with one of them. Nor—leave with one of them. Nor present one with the other's dead body. I have known from the beginning that there could be no life for any two of us—over the other's pain. I will remain with you, Soljenov, not as your bonded-weapon, but with that bonding capacity now aroused. That will be my problem. And perhaps—yours. You will let the *Enterprise* go—and you will allow the Argunovs and Z'Ehlahs to go. Then you and I will argue out the shape of our adult, until the butterfly is ready to emerge from the chrysalis.''

"No!" Kirk said, but McCoy wondered whether they all had not heard the sound of the handwriting on the wall. Was this Sola's form of the lie that *she* would be all right? Or had she seen, in fact, that McCoy's two friends were not to be hers? Not one of them, not either of them—and, God help them all, certainly not *both* of them.

"Sola," Kirk said, "you are *not* to go—'off into the night.' You, above all, have earned better than that."

Sola smiled. "I have *had* better than that, this day, from both of you. It will last me. It will have to." She turned to look for a moment at Spock. "There was one premise we did not check, Mr. Spock. And if I were of the Captain's species, and we were not on trial here, perhaps I would even check it. But in my species the answer is biological."

"What premise is that?" Spock asked.

For one moment Sola Thane's eyes lit with a kind of triumph. "The premise of monogamy, Mr. Spock."

McCoy saw Kirk and Spock trade a stunned look which he could not entirely read.

Then in the thickening silence Sola turned to Soljenov. "Now get them out of here."

Soljenov's eyes had hardened. "*Those* were not my terms," he said. "And that will not answer Gailbraith's question—will it, Gailbraith?"

"No," Gailbraith said. "It will not."

"What in God's name *is* your question?" McCoy exploded, hearing the sound of exasperation in his own voice—and the sound of terror. None of them had very long.

"I do not ask it in God's name, Doctor," Gailbraith said, "but in my own. My question has always been—oneness versus Oneness. If, as the Captain contends, there is a power of individual love which cannot be touched or equaled by Oneness—then I must at least maintain a separate Oneness and we must even learn to love. But if love does not have the power he claims for it, then we had better have Soljenov's single Totality—for nothing less will prevent chaos." He shook his head. "But mere offers to sacrifice are not sufficient. The question of love is not to be answered here."

"Yes, it *is*," Soljenov said flatly. He turned to Sola. "I will accept your counteroffer, on one condition. If that love which you profess is strong enough—and if it is really not between any two of you but among the three—if your oneness is stronger than my Oneness, there is one way to prove it. Bring both of them to you, alive, without bonding finally with either one. If you can do that, I will let them go, with their ship and their souls—and the stranger within their gates. Yes, even with your Argunovs—if they choose to go. You and I will then argue the adult."

Sola looked at the chasm yawning over the abyss. McCoy saw the slender conduit pipe by which the Vulcan might attempt a crossing to her, if there were no debilitating psionic field—and if Spock were half-ape, half-acrobat, and wholly mad. The finger- and toe-hold ledges which Kirk might attempt from his side looked even more dangerous. McCoy could sense the psionic field of the Totality, thick as glue, and moving now to focus on the two men on the ledges with—what *was* it? A kind of direct pleasure? He saw the effect strike the Vulcan, almost like pain—somehow McCoy could even sense the nature of the effect in the eddying fields of Oneness: a fiery tendril which probed at the brain centers of pleasure and then reached fiercely into the neurological centers reserved for lifelong bonds. Those bonding centers of course were strong in the Vulcan. But McCoy could also sense them surprisingly strong in Kirk. Time after time Kirk had lost someone, been held by duty to his starship, his friends, his choices in the stars. But for this love of the woman who matched him, matched them both, even the old antidote of ship and stars was not enough. Both men were open and vulnerable now, and McCoy felt Spock stiffen with resistance as the tendril probed down deeply into the brain centers which longed for pleasure and permanence. The Vulcan began to shake uncontrollably, teetering on the edge of his ledge.

Then Sola reached out to him with whatever it was she would have used for bonding. *We are one, Spock.*

But McCoy sensed that she did not cut off the thread of connection which also bound her to Kirk. Kirk also shook with the same effect. He sagged to his knees, but he spoke urgently to Spock, finding breath for it.

"Spock, go to her. *Now.* We *are* one. They won't break us, Spock. Not any of us. You *will* move, and *I* will. You were right. It *is*—we, three."

Somehow Spock lifted his head and looked across to Kirk.

"That's an order, Mr. Spock," Kirk whispered. "I'll need —your help."

Spock moved. McCoy hoped never to see a man move in that way again—and never to forget seeing this one move now. The Vulcan shook as with some aggravated neurological disorder, but he fixed his eyes on Sola and stepped out on the slender, slippery conduit. Spock moved as if summoning the power of mind over brain, bridging the neurological chaos within him by sheer will, like a cerebral-palsy victim learning to walk. But now he moved also by the pull of Sola's will, and perhaps even of Kirk's added to Spock's own.

McCoy was not altogether sure that Spock could have

walked that wire by himself, on a good day. Although you never could tell what the Vulcan could do in a pinch, especially when the pinch was closing on Kirk, among others.

Now there was certainly no way, under the assault of the mind-probe, that Spock could walk that swaying, sagging pipe. But he was doing it. From somewhere a blond young man emerged on Sola's ledge and reached out to anchor her on the edge of the ledge while she reached out to Spock. Kirk looked as if he were fused into a three-way circuit. At best there was a gap between the end of the conduit and Sola which looked as if it needed a running jump.

Then as Spock almost reached the end, his foot slipped on the slippery conduit. He fell.

McCoy's eyes wanted to lock shut, but he saw—Spock plunged toward the lava. Then somehow the Vulcan's hand caught the conduit. The pipe bent down under his weight, then sprang back up. At the top of its spring, Spock swung himself up and flung himself toward Sola—then turned loose to hurtle across fifteen feet of empty space over the abyss.

Sola's hand caught Spock's by the fingertips. He was slipping, on his way again. Then somehow they held to each other, by sheer necessity, and Spock caught the edge of the ledge and pulled himself up and in.

McCoy breathed.

For a moment the two merely held to each other at the edge of the ledge. Then they pulled apart and turned to Kirk.

Kirk's ledge was already badly eroded, and he himself looked somewhere far beyond the end of his rope. McCoy didn't even want to think about the medical toll of this day on Kirk. He would have been going on plain, raw nerve for most of it. And there was no way he was now going to traverse a narrow finger- and toe-hold ledge, in heat which should have been enough to make a Vulcan drop, and against the terrible effect of the direct pleasure. McCoy could sense that effect's power even from the periphery of the effect, and he knew the old animal research. That unremitting, unendurable pleasure would have made an animal curl up and stay with the pleasure until it died.

McCoy saw the terrible fatigue in Kirk's eyes, and the knowledge that Spock was now safely out of danger. If Kirk let himself go, Sola and Spock would be together. The

Totality would have no hold on them. And he might hope that eventually they would recover and go on.

"Jim!" McCoy called. "Don't believe it. They wouldn't make it. It *is—three.*"

McCoy saw Kirk lift his head and look at him. Then Kirk crawled to the edge and somehow slid out onto the finger- and toe-holds.

It was a mistake. Sola's control had been strained to the snapping point in helping Spock. McCoy could sense that she had almost slipped into the irrevocable two-way bonding with Spock, excluding Kirk. McCoy didn't see how she could have helped it, but it was Kirk's death warrant. He would never make it without her help against the psionic field and the lure of direct pleasure. He remained lodged on the first finger-holds, swaying out over the fire.

"Sola," McCoy said, "Spock! You both have to fight it, reach him." They didn't seem able to pull out of the effect which drew them compellingly to each other. "It's unstable," McCoy said suddenly, in the tone of swearing. "Inherently unstable, the three."

Slowly Sola turned to look at McCoy. Her tawny eyes were abstracted, as if some plan or desperation was forming in them. "No!" she countered, but her tone was desperate. She tried to reach her mind out toward Kirk and it remained with Spock.

McCoy cursed himself for a fool. How could she have been expected to know Spock as she had known him, body and stubborn Vulcan soul, and now to have brought him across that abyss—and not to cleave to him as one flesh, one soul? And how could Spock not reach back? *And they twain shall be one flesh* . . . Maybe it was always only two people who could hold each other as their highest value. And by the nature of reality if there were three, someone would always have to arrive at a point of choice, an irrevocable choice . . .

Spock moved suddenly, as if to break the hold of something which had captured him. Then he swung out on the toeholds toward Kirk.

Something seemed to snap then in Sola, and she tried to reach out mentally to Kirk—to both of them. Once again McCoy could sense effort to reestablish the three-way flow of force. Kirk shuddered and tried to inch along, like a palsy victim himself, with Spock working toward him from the other end.

But McCoy knew suddenly that he had been right. The three might conceivably get past this moment. But how would they get past the fact that there had been a life-or-death choice here, and there would be others? Somewhere there would be another choice which would have to be made finally, irrevocably and in an instant, with no chance to refuse choice.

And it might well be *now*—

McCoy felt a wrench of perspective and found himself being propelled down a hall by Gailbraith, who evidently wanted to reach the scene of the action himself—not by hologram.

McCoy sensed suddenly that Soljenov had had the same thought and was moving.

But McCoy had a terrible fear that by the time they got there, it would be over.

Chapter 32

Kirk clung to the fingerholds and could not move. For too many long seconds there he had been alone, and he had known why—and some impulse had flung him toward the Oneness. He would not burden what the other two had with his loneliness, or his mortality. Sola was reaching for him now. And Spock was coming for him. But it was too late.

Kirk found himself reaching out, not toward them, nor toward the Totality, but toward Gailbraith's Oneness. It had seemed almost a haven, once, a healing, a home. At least it was open to his choice, and not at anyone's expense . . .

'Come.'

It was Gailbraith's mind-voice, answering him.

'I will help you.'

He felt then Gailbraith's sustaining strength, fighting against the force of the Totality to protect him. Now he felt the straining of Titans against each other—over him.

And it was almost as if he felt the volcano give way further because of that. Perhaps it did. The psionic fields were powerful. They tried to rip him from the wall.

He felt Sola trying to sustain him, too. But there was some anger in him which would not answer her. He did not blame her. There was no one of her caliber who would not have had to do what she did, felt what she felt, for Spock. He had wanted that Spock, that Sola. But there was some part of Kirk which had wanted her, finally, to want only him. No. Perhaps it was more complicated than that. Perhaps he had even wanted the triangle to be—eternal.

But it was not to be.

Then suddenly she reached out to him so powerfully that he was forced to respond. She was there for him, as powerfully as she had been for Spock, lifting some weight off him. He reached and found that he could gain another handhold.

Abruptly he sensed an anger in her, too. 'I told you I could not answer for what I would feel for Spock, unchained.'

He managed to turn to look at Spock. The Vulcan was working toward him with infinite care—far more than he had taken in walking his own tightrope, The Vulcan's mind sent him strength—almost willed his fingers and toes into place for him.

But there was anger there, too. "I warned you against sacrifice," the Vulcan said through his teeth. "Especially *this* one."

Kirk did not argue, this time. Spock had made his ultimate argument on that subject, on the edge of the ledge. And then Kirk had gone ahead to defy Spock's ultimatum and had called forth Gailbraith. While Spock had come out here after him . . .

There could be some argument, Kirk decided, as to who should be mad at whom.

He could feel the pull of the Oneness now—Gailbraith was moving to reach him, reaching out ahead to guide, shelter.

There was a new universe to explore there, one he had neglected, even scorned. And it had its attractions.

He even knew that he *could* bridge the gap between Titans. Gailbraith would not join the Totality—certainly not without settling a few things with Soljenov. Soljenov would not have the three elements he needed for a galaxywide conquest. He would be forced to retrench, perhaps to argue it out with Gailbraith-Kirk if it took all millennium.

That might well be the only way to save the ship—and the galaxy—and it might be where his duty lay.

There was just one thing wrong with that, and it touched him now.

Sola and Spock reached out to him and the anger was gone, the urgency only that he live—and trust himself to their oneness, not to Oneness.

And on the toehold ledge he turned to see the Vulcan's hand stretched out to him, reaching to guide his hand to the next hold.

He reached out to the full stretch of his hand and long Vulcan fingers guided his to the next projection.

"Mr. Spock," he murmured, "you are a tower of strength and encouragement."

Chapter 33

McCoy, Gailbraith, and Dobius arrived on Sola's ledge only a moment after Soljenov, and in time to see Spock reach out to Kirk, and Kirk, after a long moment, reach back.

In the psionic field the completion of some circuit among the three was almost visible, even to McCoy. Kirk edged forward, half supported now by the Vulcan's steely hand. The toehold ledge narrowed and crumbled toward the nearer end, and Spock already seemed to be supported more by imagination than anything else.

Sola stepped out on a precarious foothold to reach out to them, but now Soljenov was moving toward her and it was plain enough that he had turned from the psionic level of the fight to some more primitive level of physical confrontation.

McCoy stepped in front of him.

Soljenov looked through McCoy as if he did not exist and seemed prepared to go straight through him—which was what, McCoy decided, he was going to have to do.

They were a foot from the edge of the ledge, and McCoy knew that he was no match for the man, let alone for the multicelled entity Soljenov actually *was*. Nevertheless, Soljenov would reach Sola and the other two over McCoy's body.

Then McCoy felt himself displaced, more or less gently, by a strength he could not begin to calculate.

He was set back against the comparative safety of the wall, and his place was taken by an Ambassador of the Federation.

For the first time Gailbraith's full power registered with McCoy, and he saw the meaning of the new species. Here was a power capable of confronting the Soljenov-Totality on its own terms, even here on its own ground.

Here was the confrontation of Titans Soljenov had predicted. And what if he was *right?* What if two or more such entities could not, for long, exist separately, and the only solution was merger to a single Oneness?

Was this the beginning of that war which would make Armageddon look like a Sunday-school picnic?

"My question has been answered," Gailbraith said.

Soljenov faced Gailbraith as if he would go through him, too. "There is no answer here," he said. "Merely a Captain who has chosen an old pattern over a new. Yet even he was tempted by Oneness. He called on *you*. My compliments. But you have not, even so, found the proper temptation."

Soljenov looked beyond Gailbraith to the three. "You contemplated going off into the Oneness alone, Captain. But in your secret heart you knew the real temptation was more than that. Sola was right. There is no solution by which the two of you can continue to love her, or she you, as singletons. There *is* a solution in Totality. Here there is room even for that love—without sacrifice. You believe you three have chosen the love and friendship which you feel for each other. You have chosen its destruction. Unless you all come to me now."

Kirk and Spock were inching along the semi-imaginary ledge, and there was no answer from them in words, but Sola spoke without turning. "We *have* chosen each other. The choice is not measured in the time we have or do not have. It is not measured at all. If we lived for a thousand years and never saw each other again, it would still have been our choice."

"That is how it will be," Soljenov said. "By our terms, if they live, you come with me."

Kirk turned sharply away from the wall. A projection crumbled under his foot and he sagged, caught only by Spock's strength. For some interval which McCoy counted in centuries they teetered above the sheer drop into the lava. Sola inched toward them along the toeholds.

McCoy saw Soljenov look at them as if he would set some last trial. He started to move toward them, and Gailbraith stopped him. They locked together, strength against strength, mind against mind, all of the power of their Many-in-One channeled to the single point of their straining bodies, the crackling contact of the two great psionic fields.

There was no room for a proper fight, but McCoy knew that he had never seen war fought in so small a space.

"They have done it," Gailbraith said through his teeth. "If individual love can survive the trials we set for it, and even the trials we did not expect, then it still has its place in the galaxy. And—we have ours. Perhaps even the butterfly can learn a lesson from the amoeba. I will not merge with you. There is friendship. Or war."

Soljenov did not answer, merely strained against him. Then McCoy saw Dobius moving in a peculiar, jerky fashion toward Sola, and he realized that the Tanian's divided brain had become the battlefield between Gailbraith and Soljenov.

Soljenov moved Dobius like a puppet and Gailbraith fought him for control. Sola was reaching for Spock where he fought to pull Kirk back in. If the big Tanian could reach them, he could help them—or pop them off the wall like beads on a string.

McCoy moved, but he would be too late.

He was not certain whether Soljenov meant to use the Tanian against the three.

For the first time it occurred to McCoy that there could be some primitive level in Soljenov which might even see Sola dead rather than let her go. Was that what some of this had been *about?* McCoy wondered. The man was the core of a new superbeing, but he was still a man who had been locked in a struggle of Titans with this single woman for years. Was it possible that he had had to know what would draw her to a man? Or what fatal flaw or error barred her to *him?*

McCoy stepped forward suddenly and caught Soljenov's eye. *"Force,"* he said. "You brought the same old error which drove you from Earth—and the one thing *she* could never accept. *Stop.* If you force this now, she will not forgive—nor *survive."*

McCoy was not certain whether he had reached Soljenov, but he had shifted some balance of attention, at least. Gailbraith's face went rigid with a massive effort. Soljenov braced against it—and the clash of mental forces seemed to make the volcano rumble still more ominously. And then Mr. Dobius' terrible efforts to move against his divided brain suddenly became smooth and easy. "Captain!" he called, and swarmed out on handholds which only his giant frame could reach.

Dobius caught Sola's hand and braced her as she drew Spock toward them, supporting an exhausted Kirk. Then the Tanian swung them past him, one by one, and at the end helped Spock support Kirk to solid ground.

The solid ground promptly began to shake. McCoy seemed to feel the volcano coming apart.

Soljenov broke away from Gailbraith and stepped back. "Doctor," he said finally, "I will consider your argument. But I do not concede your premise. Multicelled life did not regard it as force to co-opt amoebas to become a new life-form. Nor do *I*. But I now perceive that some amoebas are unsuitable for my purpose." He looked at Kirk and Spock. "And that there is some strength in—choice—which I will study."

Soljenov stepped over to Sola where she stood with Kirk and Spock. "We will go now," Soljenov said. "The volcano has perhaps four minutes to destruct. The others have gone to the escape ship. When your bargain is honored, these four may beam out."

Kirk touched Sola's shoulder, turned her to face him. "Don't go," he said.

She lifted her head. "I must."

He held her shoulders. "You have done enough. Now you deserve your reward. We—three—have just solved our immediate problem. We will solve all of it. Come with us."

Spock stepped forward quietly. "I—concur," he said.

She smiled, and McCoy saw that her eyes were bright and full. "I—cannot. I gave a word to Soljenov for your lives.

And my work is not finished. If I go, the *Enterprise* goes free, and so do the Argunovs and Z'Ehlahs among my people. And I do not believe that conquest will then be on the agenda of the Totality—when Soljenov and I have argued the shape of its adult."

Kirk turned to Soljenov. "Promise her that, *now*. Do not stand against her choice."

Soljenov shook his head. "She chose—to come with me. She is not finished—with her work or with the Totality—or perhaps even with me. Else she would not have been able to bring you through the jungles and the psionic field without bonding irrevocably to one of you."

Spock shook his head. "She could not, for other reasons."

The Vulcan turned to her. "There *is no* unsolvable problem, Sola. I am not hurt by this. Jim is not. No choice you make or do not make will harm any of the three of us. Unless—you go. I also ask you to stay."

She reached out and took Spock's hand in the Vulcan manner of paired fingers—and Kirk's in a simple clasp. "What we have had will exist—always. But it must stop here. I go. And I cannot come back. I will go *with* the Totality, not *into* it. But there are choices I must be free to make." She looked for a moment at Soljenov. "And choices I *cannot* make. While there is any danger, I cannot bond with anyone to become someone's weapon—or to give hostages to fortune. Certainly not"—for a moment her voice caught in her throat—"two hostages."

Then she stood very straight. "I did not say it, and before I lose the right: I love you, Spock."

The Vulcan started to speak, but she stopped him. "Don't say it." She turned to Kirk, "I love you, Jim, freely and forever." She leaned forward and brushed his lips.

He caught her to him, and for a moment McCoy did not think he would let her go. Then the volcano roared and spewed new lava into the chasm below.

Sola leaned away from Kirk, and McCoy did not hear but saw her lips form, "Good-bye." She caught Spock's hand to her face and then released it and turned away, blindly, to Soljenov.

Soljenov pressed a button on his belt. "Your communicator will work now, Vulcan," he said over the noise. "You have perhaps one minute."

He took Sola's arm and ran with her to the corridor opening. She stopped once and looked back—at Kirk and Spock. Then her look included McCoy for one instant. "Thank you, Doctor. Take care of them for—"

But the volcano cut off the last word.

Then she moved with Soljenov, and suddenly they were out of sight.

For a moment there was only silence, except for the threat of the volcano.

Then Kirk spoke. "The communicator, Mr. Spock."

Spock nodded and used it. "Spock to *Enterprise*. Five to beam up—immediately."

There was a sound of distance and interference, and McCoy was certain that it would not work and that they had been left to die.

Then Uhura's voice came through. "Yes, sir. We have your signal. Beaming—*now!*"

McCoy saw lava explode and splash up toward the ledge— and he heard the ungodly rumble of what must have been a thermal-powered first stage of the escape ship.

Then the transporter took them.

Chapter 34

Kirk came onto the Bridge. He moved with some difficulty, but there was no effort to it. Somewhere the gray weight of fatigue had left him—and now he was merely exhausted.

He didn't bother to conceal it from the Vulcan, or from the doctor tagging at his heels as he sank gratefully into the command chair.

"Mr. Spock, report," he said.

Spock turned from the science station to look at him. " 'On the *ship?*' " he asked.

"Certainly on the *ship*, Mr. Spock."

"The *Enterprise* is under our control again. Soljenov appears to have kept his word to release our people. Gailbraith reports them clear—and he has released those he took as a countermeasure. Mr. Dobius is unharmed. The escape ship from the volcano made it safely and is departing for Zaran."

The turbolift doors opened and Gailbraith appeared in them.

"Ambassador," Kirk said, "what are your plans? Are we to deliver you now to Zaran?"

Ambassador Gailbraith shook his head. "I intend first to report to the Federation Council—and to certain of the New Human and other Oneness groups—the results of my mission here and its implications. I shall report that the matter of choice is crucial to all such new entities, and to the galaxy. I shall also report to the Chief of Staff of Starfleet your role in bringing me to that conclusion. And I will tell him that his choice of his servant Job was—wise. Even if he did not know that I had arranged to have it made for him . . ."

"I see," Kirk said. "And have you considered who chose— Mr. Spock?"

Gailbraith smiled. "I believe *that* might have been the Devil himself." He sobered. "Gentlemen, I do offer whatever form of condolence may be appropriate. I had not foreseen that it would come to—this."

Kirk felt his jaw harden. "No. You had not. But you wished to use me, us, my ship—and her. Ambassador, I am grateful for your help in crucial matters. I applaud your decision in the matter of choice. And I would personally like to wring your neck. Would you excuse us, sir?"

Gailbraith looked at him without apology. "I would. I will look forward to dealing with you again under more propitious circumstances." He turned on his heel and left the Bridge.

Kirk sat back tiredly.

"There are still the silver birds on Vulcan," Spock said. It was the repetition of an offer he had made, long ago, when Kirk had lost Edith Keeler: the healing of Vulcan, a desert to walk on, and the bright silver birds . . .

"Thank you, Mr. Spock," Kirk said, but he shook his head. "I think—our healing is here. Whatever we have lost—I don't know about you, Spock—but I would not undo it, not any of it."

Spock was silent for a moment. "Nor I, Jim."

"The Zaran ship is accelerating, Captain," Sulu reported. "They're on their way."

McCoy came to stand close behind Kirk's chair, and for a

moment he put a hand on his shoulder. "She'll be all right, Jim."

Kirk followed the Zaran ship with his eyes. His impulse was to go after it and take the Totality on with his bare hands or bare mind—bring her back . . .

He knew he would have the impulse for a long time. And he knew that she had made her choice. Had she decided, as McCoy had said at some point, that the triangle was inherently unstable? Or had she merely gone to keep the word that had saved their lives? Or for her duty and her mission? Or for all of that, and for reasons which he might never know . . . ?

She had gone.

He would hear her voice and remember the shape of what might have been for a long time, and nevertheless, he could not regret that she had come.

He looked at Spock, and it seemed to him that the chains and the vultures had lifted. The look of control was merely deeper and more certain now. And he did not think that the Vulcan would ever regret this day, either.

One day perhaps they would have to tackle the issue of Oneness head-on. But for the moment Kirk would settle for the particular amoebas he had around him. And for the memory of one who had come, and gone.

"Heading for home, Mr. Sulu," he said. "Warp Factor Three. Let's go."

LEGACY

A routine survey of the planet Alpha Octavius Four turns disastrous as Spock is attacked and poisoned by a huge creature and Kirk's landing party is trapped underground by a violent earthquake. As Spock fights for his life in sick bay, Scotty organises a search for Kirk and his men. However, rescue efforts must cease when the *Enterprise* is called away to the Beta Cabrini system where a mining colony is under heavy attack.

At Beta Cabrini, the *Enterprise* faces off against a Marauder named Dreen - a man that Spock had watched his former captain Christopher Pike defeat years before. Fighting the effects of the poison, Spock struggles to his feet and takes command of the ship. Soon, Spock and Dreen are locked into a deadly game of cat and mouse - a game driven by mad revenge that can have only one survivor!

Coming soon from Titan Books
The exciting sequel to Dreadnought!

BATTLESTATIONS!

Back on Earth enjoying a well-deserved shore leave, Captain Kirk is rudely accosted by a trio of Starfleet Security guards. It seems he is wanted for questioning in connection with the theft of transwarp - the Federation's newest, most advanced propulsion system. Could Captain Kirk, Starfleet's most decorated hero, be guilty of stealing top-secret technology? With the aid of Mr. Spock, Lt. Cmdr. Piper begins a desperate search for the scientists who developed transwarp - a search that leads her to an isolated planet, where she discovers the real - and very dangerous - traitor!

STAR TREK:
THE NEXT GENERATION NOVELS

0: ENCOUNTER AT FARPOINT

1: GHOST SHIP

2: THE PEACEKEEPERS

3: THE CHILDREN OF HAMLIN

4: SURVIVORS

5: STRIKE ZONE

6: POWER HUNGRY

7: MASKS

8: THE CAPTAINS' HONOUR

9: A CALL TO DARKNESS

10: A ROCK AND A HARD PLACE

11: GULLIVER'S FUGITIVES

12: DOOMSDAY WORLD

13: THE EYES OF THE BEHOLDERS

14: EXILES

15: FORTUNE'S LIGHT

16: CONTAMINATION

17: BOOGEYMEN

Coming soon:

18: Q IN LAW

STAR TREK:
THE NEXT GENERATION GIANT NOVELS

METAMORPHOSIS

VENDETTA

For a complete list of Star Trek publications, T-shirts and badges please send a SAE to Titan Books Mail Order, Panther House, 38 Mount Pleasant, London, WC1X 0AP. Tel: (071) 833 3777.
Please quote reference ST49.